RAG PICKERS

UNIVERSITY OF CALGARY
Press

RAG PICKERS

BLAINE NEWTON

Brave & Brilliant Series
ISSN 2371-7238 (Print) ISSN 2371-7246 (Online)

University of Calgary Press
2500 University Drive NW
Calgary, Alberta
Canada T2N 1N4
press.ucalgary.ca

LIBRARY AND ARCHIVES CANADA CATALOGUING IN PUBLICATION

Title: Rag pickers / Blaine Newton.
Names: Newton, Blaine, author.
Series: Brave & brilliant series ; no. 43.
Description: Series statement: Brave & brilliant series, 2371-7238 ; no. 43
Identifiers: Canadiana (print) 20250108836 | Canadiana (ebook) 20250108844 | ISBN
    9781773856186 (hardcover) | ISBN 9781773856193 (softcover) | ISBN 9781773856209 (PDF)
    | ISBN 9781773856216 (EPUB)
Subjects: LCGFT: Short stories.
Classification: LCC PS8627.E955 R34 2025 | DDC C813/.6—dc23

The University of Calgary Press acknowledges the support of the Government of Alberta
through the Alberta Media Fund for our publications. We acknowledge the financial support
of the Government of Canada. We acknowledge the financial support of the Canada Council
for the Arts for our publishing program.

Printed and bound in Canada by Imprimerie Gauvin
This book is printed on Enviro paper

Editing by Naomi K. Lewis
Cover image: Colourbox #3954040
Cover design, page design, and typesetting by Melina Cusano

For Leslie

CONTENTS

A Life Indivisible

It was on a Tuesday when the rain finally came after a long drought — the same Tuesday when he began to suspect that critical events in his life always happened in years when his age was a prime number.

Clearly *one* is not prime, but a fundamental unit — a building block. Accordingly, it had been nothing but a series of new and interesting things: walking, words, the primary functions of sustainable life — all conveyed to him by others: parents and observers, and by the unimpeachable testimony of family snapshots. But by the ages of two and three, prime numbers both, he had begun to dabble in awkward self-awareness, had begun to take ownership of his own stories.

Five brought school; seven a first kiss. Eleven, an awakening of his understanding that the rivalries and violence inherent in the schoolyard extended to the larger world. Thirteen, puberty; seventeen, beer, high school graduation, university and a first love won then lost. Nineteen, sex; twenty-three, a wife; twenty-nine, a child; thirty-one, the loss of his child; thirty-seven a divorce; forty-one, the accident that claimed his parents.

Until his forty-third birthday, when he found himself reaching for the door of an art gallery in order to escape a sudden and unforecast downpour.

The route was one he'd often followed on his way from his small third floor walk-up to his job (before he lost his job — a birthday surprise he hadn't anticipated — the HR representative sincerely awkward for once, escorting out the newly redundant actuary with the cake stain on his lapel and the party hat on his head).

He must have passed this door countless times, perhaps even glanced at the art on display in the windows, but he'd never entered. Now, as he shook off the rain, smoothed back his wet hair, a woman approached with a glass in hand.

"Glad you could make it," she said, in a practiced tone. She was taller than he by several inches, although that may have been due to her heels, and younger by several years, although that could have been a trick of the gallery light. "This nasty weather seems to have kept people away in droves," she continued. Clearly, she meant this as some kind of joke, because she smiled — a rather pleasant smile he thought — then seemed embarrassed by his silence.

The building was old — a brick exterior that had been red once, but now was darkened by soot, like a warning to other buildings of the danger of secondhand smoke. Exposed brick of a healthier nature formed the interior perimeter walls to a point a third of the way up, the remainder of the high walls white with dark wood trim along the ceiling edge. Or so it seemed, from what little he'd seen, for so far he had stepped in only enough to allow the door to swing closed. He returned his gaze to her, then surmised, from the silence punctuated only by the sighing of a radiator catching its breath, that they were alone.

"It's period paintings and photographs," she continued. "Local artists — work from the late forties and early fifties. Some more modern. Some older." Again a pause. "May I offer you a glass of wine?"

She gestured towards a nearby table. Sitting on the white tablecloth were a dozen or so bottles of moderately priced red and white wine — domestic, perhaps in keeping with the art — attended by two neat rows of stemmed glasses.

"If you don't have one I can't and, well, it's been a little slow." She glanced down at the glass in her hand, then slowly back at him, and he was uncertain whether it had been recently emptied or only just picked up.

"Red, please." She turned away, and he stepped from the foyer into the room. It smelt of varnish and dust.

"These are mostly pen-and-ink with one or two charcoal," she said, assuming a question he never anticipated as she offered a glass of red wine and gestured vaguely to the small prints framed and matted in black lining the walls at eye level. Most were no larger than a laptop, some as small as a playing card. A white wine was her choice. "The room through this door is oils and watercolours. Through that door are the photographs. The three rooms are connected — it's a circuit." She handed him a coloured piece of paper, apparently as a guide. "Clockwise or counterclockwise — left or right — it's your choice. We don't profile."

"What is — is this — a showing? An install?" he asked, turning the paper over in his hand.

"An installation?"

"Yes." He hadn't yet taken the offered glass, but now he reached out, if for no other reason than to avoid her look of disappointment.

"Oh. You're here by accident."

"The rain . . ."

"Of course. Ah. Well. I should just be glad there's someone else in the building. They told me there was a ghost, but you can't even rely on them anymore."

She turned away, but his sudden guilt caused a guttural noise she must have mistaken for him clearing his throat in preparation to speak, for she turned back, an expectant look on her tilted face.

"I — I don't really know much about art," he offered by way of apology.

"This isn't a test."

Another joke? He inhaled and plunged once more into the conversation.

"I mean — I don't really know what I'm supposed to be looking at — for — at."

She held his look for a moment before making a soft exhalation and turning her gaze down to her wineglass.

"I suppose you're about to say you don't know 'what you like.'"

"Yes. Uh, no. Uh —" her eyes again met his. They were green, he saw, with what he suspected were flecks of brown, and he found he wanted to step closer to verify.

"Relax. Breathe. Take a sip of your wine — it's really much more mediocre than the flashy label on the bottle would suggest."

He followed her advice — a sip then a breath — and thought he could catch her scent of cinnamon and flowers through the wine's overtones of berries and chocolate. He felt better, calmer.

"Come on," she continued. "I'll give you a little tour. It'll be something for me to do until the busload of Japanese tourists arrives."

"I'm not good with crowds —" but he stopped as she again held his look — this time for several languid seconds — breaking it at last with a smile that told him that, no, in fact, there would be no bus tour and no tourists. They would be alone. And this made him happy.

Or maybe it was the way she took his hand, leading him like a child as she said, "Let's start in the middle and leave our options open," her wine hand casually snagging an open bottle of white as she passed the table and moved on through the archway to the adjacent room. He did the same with an open bottle of red, noting several screw caps delinquent in the corner.

This room was different. The red brick ran higher up and seemed to have been deliberately broken, smashed from the outer walls in chunks, leaving jagged lines, and rubble piled against two support columns in the middle of the room like cairns. The feel was one of active and energetic entropy.

She released his hand, crossed to the far wall, and sat on the floor, her feet out in front of her.

"No furniture, I'm afraid. Not a single chair. Function sacrificed for form." She smoothed out her skirt, an almost sepia colour, as if chosen by a camouflage expert to blend with the patinated wood of the floor. She patted the space next to her as she nudged off her shoes and rubbed the bottom of her left foot with the side of her right. He joined her, placing the bottle next to him on the ancient hardwood.

"Keep a close eye on the bottle. This floor hasn't been level since the day it was first laid."

"Is that a joke?"

"Perhaps. I'll leave you to sift for it. You seem to have a knack." Again she smiled in that way he was finding increasingly comforting, and took a not insubstantial sip of her wine. He copied.

"This," she swept her free hand across the room, "is the photographic display — my favourite. The others are too artificial." He nodded his head, without understanding. "I know I'm supposed to be selling this shit, and I know I should have a deep appreciation for all art forms, and I don't really mind painters reinventing reality, but you should at least be able to see where reality once hung its hat. Reality is not an ex-husband to be snipped from the wedding album. Here, though, it's different. Here it's the unflinching eye of the camera."

He looked back through the archway where he thought he could spy the ankle of an empty bottle under the skirt of the table cloth, then took in the room in a slow arc — framed photographs, of varying sizes, most snapshots in small groupings.

"Are they all —?"

"The same artist? Good question. And not as easy to answer as you might think. No."

"No."

"Correct. Now comes the tricky bit." He took another drink, independently this time. "One artist compiled the photographs, but they're from a wide range of photographers."

"I don't —"

"Yes. Confusing, I imagine. This building was once was a photo studio. It closed down in '83, and the place has been mostly empty since. Sad, really. Such a grand old building left to the savage whims of time, like an aging *grande dame* sitting at a bus stop."

"In the rain."

"Yes," she laughed, and he felt a kiss of joy, "in the rain. During renovations last year, they found boxes in a back storeroom. Envelopes full of old photographs. The best we can figure, they were developing orders that were never picked up."

He rose and moved slowly to a wall.

"Isn't that —?"

"Theft? Breach of copyright? Plagiarism? The artist didn't think so, and who are we to judge? There was no way to track down the owners — no phone numbers or addresses on the envelopes — or the few that had numbers were long ago out of service. She cropped some photos, colourized a few more, combined others in the same frame. Artistic license, it's called. Or, at least, she called it."

She topped up her glass and then watched his slow circuit of the room. He moved to each frame in a clock-like rhythm, rising onto his toes or bending his knees as necessary so that each was seen from the same direct perspective, from the same distance. Then he stopped suddenly, moved two pictures back, and pointed with the brochure in his hand.

The picture was of a park: long sloping green leading to the water's edge. A lake, it seemed, or a calm but substantial river. A few trees stood in the foreground, while in the back was a smudged line of grey reaching into a white sky.

One man stood with a group of gentlemen. Four wore bowler hats and dark jackets of a style consistent with the turn of the last century. Only he, the fifth, stood in shirt sleeves. Only he wore a slight smile, and not the serious expression of one who suspects they're being somehow immortalized. His look was of one who knows that the present is more important than immortality — the cold beer he has just enjoyed, the women just out of view of the camera.

The man's forearms and face had been colourized to a deep tan. His hair was dark — straight but unruly, as if just ruffled by a recent breeze or a friendly hand. An untrimmed moustache gloated above a bemused mouth.

She slid forward, onto her knees, watching.

"Do you know —"

"The photographer? No. It's the oldest pictures they found. 1907, maybe."

She rose and stood next to him. He noticed, with her shoes off, he matched her height.

"This," he finally said, by way of introduction, "is my grandfather. Harold. Harold —"

"Emma," she replied.

"And I'm Alan."

Emma removed the picture from the hook and released a security clip. Alan gently took it and turned to the centre of the room.

"Strange," she offered. "He was twenty-something then? He'd be well over a hundred now."

"One hundred and seventeen. He died twenty-nine years ago."

"I'm sorry," she replied, startled at how automatically it came. "Did you — did you know him well? Were you close?"

"Yes."

The frame felt heavy in Alan's hands, causing him to sit where he stood. He placed the picture face up on the floor.

"What are the odds, huh?" Emma knelt opposite him, observing the photograph upside down. "A handsome man. Do you know the picture?"

"No."

"Maybe it looks different — the artist may have manipulated it."

"No."

"Is there someone else who needs to —"

"There's no one else."

The energy of the picture would not reconcile with the shadow of the antique man he knew, less alive than this shadow on film.

Alan at thirteen — his last visit to that curtained room — the room with no pictures, no connection with the outside world. The smell of staleness. His father staring out the window to the littered alley, a cup of stale coffee in his hand. Harold asleep in the armchair by the bed, a dark green terry towel robe rumpled around his gaunt frame. The intervals between fragmented conversations, shards of stories and broken words piled like the bricks in this room. His father's nods filling in for words. Harold's struggle to surface, to connect, to be free from the shell that held his life, to feel again the wind, Alan now knew, and the joy of ill-considered choices made in the warmth of a weekend sun.

Alan touched for a moment his own prudent choices. There was no one to tell of this find because he and fate had conspired to insulate him from anyone who might listen. He thought of his own room now — his small apartment, void of outside connection. The window that overlooked a parking lot. Grey light. Shadows of neighbours.

"I'd like to —"

He looked to Emma, unsure of what he had said — of when he had started to speak, but she seemed to know. The smile she wore was now more subdued, more subduing, making him feel safe.

"Yes —?" she encouraged.

"I'd like to —" He waited for her to finish his sentence, as she had done before, as he now wanted her to do. But she was quiet. Waiting. "I'd like to — to take this home —"

A brief sadness swept across her eyes before she pointed to a small card on the wall next to where the picture had hung, with a price discreetly marked. He fumbled with his wallet, dropping his credit card on the floor. She picked it up with a practiced sweep as she rose, then collected her shoes and moved to the first room. He followed without prompting. From a small table she picked up the card reader, a receipt book, a pen.

"Art is always a wise investment. You never know which piece will appreciate. They all do, but some more so. A sudden shift in tastes — or when the artist dies."

"Is she old?"

"Twenty-three. But her life choices are largely high risk." She offered him yet another smile as she swept his card through the machine, handed both to him, and began to write out the receipt.

He turned to the outside window. The rain had now stopped. The steady roar of the earlier downpour had been replaced by the irregular cadence of drips through torn awnings. The sky was still grey, blending with the surrounding buildings, softening their edges. He looked back through the door to where they had sat

— the wine bottles in the middle of the floor like sentinels, casting shadows in multiple ratios to the overhead lights.

She finished writing and stood ready to tear the receipt free, but when he failed to respond to her wordless cue she seemed to freeze, looking at him, as if he, too, were a photograph. He felt a momentary panic, a brief loss of context. He could feel his heart racing, his temperature rise uncomfortably. Then the plummet back to the moment.

"Oh." He punched in a number and offered back the machine. With a whir and a tear of paper, time was urged forward, receipts written and printed, the picture wrapped for travel — his brief feeling that she held onto it a little longer than was necessary, tugging him slightly towards her before releasing.

"I guess — I should probably — there's really —"

"Yes. Nothing to keep you here. The rain has stopped. The tide has turned. The ark is now boarding, please have picture ID ready."

"Yes. Thank you." He handed her the brochure. "Perhaps someone else —"

"Someone else —" she repeated, with what he hoped was a kind of sadness.

With that he pushed through the door and stepped back onto the sidewalk. He looked back through the window, seeing her slow return into the gallery, her form framed by the doorway, sepiaed by the tinted glass and the stream of water still finding equilibrium and the low lights pushing against the grey.

He glanced at the receipt and noted on the line for a clerk name she had dotted the *i* of her last name with a heart — also that the business number had been stroked out and a new one written in, but the new phone number didn't match the one on the shop door. He looked up again, but she was gone from view, as was her wine bottle, and he turned to walk home.

But it would be several hours later, as he prepared to hang the picture over the desk in his bedroom and the receipt fluttered from its temporary home in the brown paper wrapping, before he realized that the new phone number, divided as area code, prefix and suffix, formed three distinct prime numbers.

THE TEA RITUAL

It sometimes seemed to me as if, when I slept, the world, or at least my world, was disassembled, only to be reassembled in the morning by forces unknown. But sometimes, especially if I was disturbed or awakened suddenly in the small hours, it did not come together correctly, like an IKEA project with a missing piece and no pictogram guide to put it right.

She looked as if she'd been up for hours — had dressed up especially for that moment — in a pale cream dress with a light blue pattern of wavy lines, with a paler blue cardigan over top. Her hair was up. I couldn't see if she was wearing shoes, but I knew she must be. It would only be proper.

Maybe old people don't sleep. It was a little after three a.m. I was in my pajamas — the new ones Beth had given me, the ones with the broad blue stripes. My frayed robe was open, the belt ends draping like a vine, bare feet on the cold wood floor, a water glass in hand, watching her from my building opposite. This was the third night.

I normally slept well. Eight solid hours without fail. Anything less and I'm sluggish during the day. My concentration is ragged and I'm irritable, and my tolerance of my coworkers becomes grudging.

But three nights ago Beth and I had a fight. Same thing. When are we going to set a date? Why am I afraid to commit? I'm twenty-eight; when am I going to stop acting like a selfish child? It ended abruptly. She hung up. Typical. She'd called back a couple of times since, but I saw the number and didn't pick up. I needed time to think — about rational things like finances and logistics, equity and tax implications — but all I could think about was how she was always bossing me around, how she pushed me constantly, how she hummed tuneless songs and always bought the same fancy tinned soup with squash and carrot but never ate it, and how light through a window would wrap around her as if it were an accessory of fashion, part of what defined her.

I'd spent several hours in bed staring at the ceiling, then several more in broken, dreamful sleep, finally awake again with a gasp and tug in my chest, my mouth dry. I'd gotten up for a glass of water. Stumbled along on in the dark. There was enough light from the moon and the street lamp outside to navigate, I thought, what with my vague recollection of the placement of furniture in my apartment, prompted by hints from my shins.

As I moved back through the living room, I stopped at the window. No particular reason. Boredom. To see what the weather was like. To glimpse this other world I never saw, that seemed to function so well without me. The night had always seemed a mystery to me: it wasn't the past, fading out of reach, and it wasn't the future still to come, but a present of no meaning, void of light or depth.

She was one floor down, to the right. The only apartment lit. Three windows, open to the heat. The nearest looked to me like a kitchen. I could see some cabinets, a sink, a small table with two chairs. The other two windows opened to a living room or a dining room, probably combined, as some of these older buildings have. There were bookshelves, a writing desk (the old kind with a door that swings down to make the writing surface), a chair that looked like faded oxblood leather.

It wasn't as if the lights in her apartment were blazing. A lamp in the living room was on, and a ceiling light in the kitchen. These were enough to show soft yellow edges against the backdrop of the dark building — a building that had always blended with the rest of the block during the day, and I wouldn't have noticed anything tonight if I'd turned my own lights on. But surrounded by dark, so close to the window as I was, it presented to me a show of sorts.

From the first night her routine was always the same, but I couldn't have known that. The first night I just happened to notice this white-haired woman — walking from her kitchen to the living room, disappearing for a moment then reappearing in the next window, framed like she was moving between two computer screens.

I shouldn't really have cared. I couldn't recall ever seeing her before in the neighbourhood, but I wondered. I turned away and took a few steps back from the window to return to bed — to invest again in sleep, finally — but I wondered what she could be doing at this hour, dressed like she was about to go out shopping or visit a friend. So I turned back — returned to my window — watched for the few minutes as she walked through her room, touched this or that object, then exited stage left into what I guessed was a hallway, out of view, and the lights went off. Even so, I remained at my window for at least another half hour, feeling my erratic breathing, a foreign restlessness.

I don't know why the next night brought me back — why I awoke so suddenly, as if by alarm but earlier this time. I hadn't given her a second thought that day. I hadn't thought of her as I went to bed that night. I'd fallen into a deep sleep quickly, back to my usual routine, all cares sloughed. But I awoke shortly after two, feeling as if my breath were out of reach across the room, with a firm vision of her at her window.

She was sitting at the kitchen table this time, alone, a small cup in front of her. I never saw her drink from it, just turn it on the saucer with the fingertips of both hands, looking down as if considering the ripples and waves.

She was dressed much as the night before, casual but proper, not old-fashioned, but not up to date. The clothes were more practical than classic, the colours subdued. After a few minutes, she rose and put the cup and saucer in the sink. Facing the window now, as she rinsed and dried the china, I could see something of her face despite the distance and the low light.

Her hair was white, her face oval. As she finished her task and turned, something of her slightly shuffling step and the merest of stoops spoke to me of age. Maybe eighty? But what do I know? My own parents have been gone for years and neither lived much beyond sixty. And in the haste of my days, it's not like I've made a study of the grey-hairs around me.

But she began to move through the next room following a system that didn't change in any substantive way from night to night. A pattern — always from left to right as I observed it. She would enter from the kitchen, after her tea and after washing and drying the single cup and saucer, pick up a small object from the living room hutch, hold it, observe it for several long seconds, then place it back down and progress through the room, move to a second object and then a third, then a fourth. Sometimes her face was visible to me, often not, and, although I strained to see, I never saw her lips move — I never had a feeling she was saying anything — that she was speaking, for the benefit of herself or another, either present or not. But still, I had the impression of a ritual, of a sequence thought out and considered, and of some importance.

This sequence would take less than an hour — never precisely the same, from my limited observation, but never significantly in variance, before she would disappear — before the lights would go out, reducing the building to darkness, shifting my focus to the shadowed texture of the bricks now seen through my hollow reflection, and I would take a sudden breath, turn away, and return to my bed with a feeling of restfulness and restlessness in equal measure.

I watched her for three nights. By the third I had a growing feeling of peacefulness as I watched her circuit, her routine, her ritual. But there was a small change that suddenly unsettled me. At the far right of the room, just an object or two from what would have been the conclusion, she turned to the window and looked in my direction. She didn't move. She held in her hands a framed picture of some kind, faced to her. I froze, afraid to move, afraid a sweep of traffic light or a movement of a curtain had betrayed my vantage. But after a moment, she turned back, placed down the frame, ran a light finger over its top, and left the room. Soon the light was off.

On the fourth night she wasn't there. Or the fifth or the sixth, although I stood at my window for over an hour — well before and after our allotted time. By this time I had phoned Beth — told her I would be out of town on business for I didn't know how long — that I would call her when I got back. She accepted my lie without believing — knowing, I'm sure, that it was part of my own pattern.

On the morning after the seventh night I left my building early to walk to work, breaking my routine by a half-hour, stepping out onto a sidewalk bright with morning sun. Across the street, in front of the woman's building, a crowd had formed — a few dozen people — with an ambulance, silent but with lights flashing and the rear door open, waiting.

I approached an older woman in a bright kerchief, who seemed to be actively engaged with the others — moving among them — her eyes bright, her face expressive, touching some on the shoulder as she leaned in to deliver a shard of information.

"What happened?" I asked.

"Mrs. Griffin — 3G — she's dead," she said, turning to me, eager to show her command of the moment.

"3G? Third floor? Front? Corner?"

"Yes. No one had heard boo from her in four or five days."

"Four or five —"

"Super went in," she continued. "She was dead, poor dear. Been there for days. Imagine. Days." I thought I could see the glimmer of a smile on her face, a certain joy in providing news of such sadness and regret.

"But the ambulance?"

"Oh, they have to come. They have to be the ones who move the body. After the police are done. Procedure. I know. I've seen it — on TV," she clarified.

"Police?"

I looked up, saw the squad car, lights flashing in an unsynchronized rhythm with the ambulance in the foreground. As I turned back, the crowd made a collective shift as the doors to the building opened and two paramedics carried a stretcher down the steps. The body was covered fully. Still, it seemed too small — so insignificant — as if they were removing waste and not a person.

She had not been seen for four or five days. She had no reason to be out. She may have spent her last days in silent circuits of her few rooms.

"So sad," the woman continued, though more engaged with the progress of the stretcher than any real sense of sympathy. "Mister's been dead several years now, before she moved here. The children — two, I think — live in another city. I don't think they've visited for a while. No friends. Well, at ninety . . ." She finished with a look to me — to complete in my own mind what might have been an insensitive observation about death and statistical inevitability and the sadness of being last. "I wonder —" and again she left me to do her dirty work of supposition — the hows and whys that must circle any lonely death, any last minutes alone.

Soon the moment was broken. The ambulance pulled away — no lights now, no siren, nothing to herald their package — to signal any need for right-of-way or acknowledgements or hatless nods of deference. I wouldn't have been surprised if their first stop was to a drive-through for a couple of lattes to go.

Two police officers appeared at the top of the steps. The larger of the two took two steps down.

"We need you to move along, folks. There's nothing more here."

But the crowd had started to break up even before the first sentence was complete. There *was* nothing more here. Time to move on, like strays to chase the next stink.

Alone on the sidewalk with the kerchiefed woman, I looked up to where the lady would have been, surprised at how different the building looked from this perspective — the sharp upward angle, the infrequent decorative grotesques on the building face focused out on nothing in particular, grinning in a way I found unsettling.

"Did you know her?"

"No. I'd seen her around, occasionally," I replied (a truth, or a lie grown from the same stock), my focus still upward. I'd seen her, sure, but never before the window and never anywhere else that I could recall. I may well have passed her a thousand times, though. I nodded to the kerchiefed woman, by way of a goodbye, to continue my journey, but she was already moving to the officers.

I'm almost thirty, and I've done a lot of things in my relatively short life — some things that I'm proud of, some things I'd rather not have colleagues recite at the open mic at my funeral, and what seems like an infinite number of things that don't make a good goddamn bit of difference to anyone but seemed necessary to me at the time to inch me to where I am today, where ever that is: a job I could do in my sleep in a city with which I have no connection, except for Beth. But in that time — in that lifetime — I had never broken into an apartment. Certainly not the apartment of a recently deceased stranger — which is where I found myself on the 8th night.

Although I knew she couldn't be there, I was once again up at two, looking across to where I expected her, where I wanted her to be — knowing this made no sense — until my jacket and keys were in my hand and I was moving down the stairs, across the street, through the unlocked glass door and into her building — and I was standing outside of 3G at a little before three in the morning, unsure what to do next.

The door was a dark wood and seemed solid. The numbers brass and thick. There was one deadbolt lock, brass, Yale. The doorknob itself, also brass, looked original to the building — a shiny and uneven patina, smooth from years of use. It turned easily, telling me that there was only the deadbolt to deal with. I leaned against the door, gave it a brief push. It was ungiving, as I knew it would be, and pushed back against me with a loud clunk that caused me to look around to the nearest other door up the corridor.

In my jacket pocket was a large flat-head screwdriver — part of a toolkit I'd picked up back when I'd bought into the belief that men should be able to fix the things they own, otherwise they're not really theirs. I'd grabbed the screwdriver as I left with an unthinking surety. This was the first time I'd used it.

I inserted the head between the lock and the doorjamb and leaned against it to leverage the door back on its hinges, crush a localized piece of the wooden jamb just a little to allow the bolt to spring free — as I'd seen on TV — believing with the undying faith of the constant viewer that the door would just pop open to my will. But it didn't. As I pondered this lack of physics understanding in my life, and the betrayal of my cable upbringing, I noticed there were scratches in the metal and small nicks in the wood. Looking more closely, I could imagine clearly an ancient hand that was unsteady with a key, a mind unsteady with memory — and the logical result that a key must be stashed somewhere in the hallway just in case.

Fingertips along the top of the door found nothing, but I saw there was a large plant at the end of the corridor, just a few feet away by the window, in a ceramic pot on a wooden stand. When I turned the pot, a brass key winked at me from the damp soil at the back. I was surprised at the ease — the lack of security — the success of the simplest of guesses by the simplest of burglars.

The lock surrendered without complaint, and the door swung open six or seven inches with no revealing squeak or groan. I gathered the shards of my composure and moved quickly inside, closing the door.

There was little light — fragments from the same streetlight that I've relied upon so many times. The room smelt of flowers and furniture polish, lemon and seven types of tea, and looked inviting, as if it had been cleaned in preparation — as if visitors were always welcome, day or night.

My hesitation to turn on a light was countered with the reductive logic that my apartment was empty — and of the few others that lived opposite this one who might see me, how many would actually know I didn't belong here if they did see me — and how many of those would still be up at this hour to see anything at all? And how many could be bothered to look? I moved to the kitchen and turned on the light; the sudden brightness a physical presence.

A tea cup and saucer waited on the table — at the place where I had seen her sit just nights earlier — a smallish china cup, white, with a design of purple thistles — the blooms on long, leaved stems of green winding about the cup. A small silver spoon stood guard next to the cup and saucer: a commemorative spoon from a distant coronation. A sugar bowl matching the cup design sat in the middle of the table. On the counter was a kettle, plugged in, a china tea pot of a separate design from the cup, a small canister of looseleaf tea — an oolong. All was in place. She had set it all out in readiness for her use. I switched on the kettle, drummed my fingers on the counter, then turned and moved down a dark hallway.

In the bedroom, the bed was unmade, the sheets half on the floor. A torn nightdress was discarded beneath the window — a side window that looked onto the brick wall of the adjacent building. This must have been where they found her, the paramedics, in bed. I imagined the scene, brisk but unrushed, the nightdress torn away to permit examination — to ensure efficiency of procedure — torn out of an adherence to protocol and not necessity. There were no clothes about — nothing draped on a chair. Of course not. She would neatly fold them, or hang them in the closet each night, or place them carefully in a laundry hamper discreetly located.

The nearest closet door revealed rows of clothes: blouses, skirts hung full length, not folded, the spacing even and uncrowded. The adjacent closet, almost empty, held a single man's suit, dark, and a lone tuxedo. Both perfect. Two pairs of shined shoes lined up below like memories. The top shelf crammed with photo albums, labelled with the span of years. I reached up and touched one lightly, afraid it will burst open with lost moments. It was smooth and clean and cool.

Closing the door, I turned back to the room, expecting the cliché chalk outline or police tape, but she didn't warrant this. She would have found the fuss somehow distasteful, I'm sure. There was nothing but a double bed, the dark wood of the headboard with carved scrolls and rosettes, the matching end tables each with a small lamp and beige shade, a vanity and dresser, a small-backed red plush chair with embroidered cushion. It was a set for a period play, awaiting the actors to enter and the curtain to rise.

On the left end table was a small book, soft leather bound — love poems, I saw when I opened it, the flyleaf inscribed "To Sarah, my love. Bob," a single piece of clover pressed on the back leaf. Next to it in a simple wooden frame a black-and-white picture of a handsome man in a dark suit, a pipe in hand. The same pipe sat next to it.

On the right table was a triptych — the photos of three children: a boy of perhaps twelve, a girl around thirteen. Both were smiling: the boy squinting into the light with an energetic grin, the girl with familiar eyes and a knowing confidence. The middle photo was another boy, perhaps ten. This one had a small newspaper clipping taped to the glass. A death notice. I touched the brittle paper but did not read it.

On the dresser, along with a brush and two small cut glass bottles with silver tops, sat a child's toy. A race car — old, bullet-shaped, tin, with faded paint, cracked rubber wheels. A remembrance, perhaps — the lost child or a young brother.

The kettle's whistle called to me. Back in the kitchen I placed the black tea in the strainer, warmed the pot as my mother had once taught me, poured the water, waited the four minutes for the loose leaves to unfold. In the refrigerator I found a china jug of milk — "never cream for tea," I heard my mother's voice, and almost turned to where she might be. Sugar cubes were in the bowl, with silver tongs for the delicate work of sweetening. Soon I was seated at the table, a cup of milky, sweet tea, stirring it slowly with the silver spoon, two clockwise movements, then two counterclockwise, the spoon never touching the cup.

The first sip took me back, to distant days and a different city that seemed far on the other side of the world, though in fact only a few hours by car. The hot tea almost burnt my throat — "best to drink it as hot as you can stand it" — and the recollection caused a tightening in my chest as if resurfacing too quickly.

I rose, cup in hand, and moved into the living room. So small, of an age where just a chair and a fireplace and a newspaper spelt comfort. No TV, I noticed. The fireplace now held a small electric heater fashioned to look like a coal fire. One wall had five or six painting, rural scenes mostly, one of a wooden country church, gravestones in the foreground. Originals, the signature was legible as R Griffin. Robert. Bob.

On the mantel was a brass clock under a glass cover — an anniversary clock, they're called. A small engraved plaque celebrated forty years and identified it was a gift from a church group many years earlier. A single standing lamp cast uneven light over a room sparse of furniture but crowded with things. Porcelain figurines in bright colours — ladies of the court and their dandies. Small spoons with images of vacations spots hung on the wall in a walnut box. A brass key on frayed twine. Curios now detritus.

The single leather chair sat to one side, next to a small table and lamp. A second, smaller chair was angled next to it, close enough that a hand could reach across to touch the arm of another. Doilies — is that what they call them, those linen rectangles with delicate fringes — rested on the back of the chairs. My mother used to use these for when Uncle Charlie visited — to keep his hair oil from staining the chair — the hair he used to colour and pomade well into his sixties.

A cabinet against the far wall was filled with china tea cups — visible through the glass of the door. All are mismatched — lone cup and saucer pairings — and I remembered a story my mother once told me — the custom in her small prairie town of the women giving the new bride china — each giving the bride-to-be a cup and saucer in a different pattern — to represent the different characters of each — as reminder of community and the need for 'teas' to keep the community together — connected — as if their souls were contained in the bone white.

On the wall was a small plate — a commemorative — with the name of a community far from here — Balmoral — and the date of its centennial, now many years in the past. The sense of distance and time was palpable, like the smoky taste of the tea, the tick of the mantel clock. I touched some items, spent a moment looking at others.

A cluster of small photographs near the archway showed older scenes — posed stances of past ages. Couples. Parents, grandparents, I assumed, continued a procession down the hallway. Photographs from a time when pictures were few and precious. Not like today, when we select a moment by sorting through hundreds of perfected digital versions.

Then the comment the kerchief lady had made came back to me. That she was alone. That no one visited. The children in distant cities. And I realized every item in this room — every cup and trinket — had no longer any real connection to anyone else. The chain had been broken, the thread snagged and pulled to unravelling. The children would come in and deal with the details — the boxing up, the disposal — with most of it becoming something for charities or yard sales. A life bartered for loose change on a cloudy weekend.

A night breeze moved the curtain, with the smell of rain. The windows were still open from the warm night several days back. I closed the windows, then moved back to the kitchen.

At that window I looked out, found my own apartment, the window where I had stood. I expected to see my own shadow, as my spectral self judged me from one story up and slightly to the side. There was nothing, of course. Only darkness. The distant sound of sparse traffic below, a siren somewhere.

A phone rang muffled, somewhere, then stopped, answered by someone unheard through the apartment wall. I turned and moved through the archway, down the short hallway that led again to the bedroom. I smelled again the flowers and hairspray (a genteel scent that spoke to me of age and custom, of expectation of what is right). Now I saw that everywhere on the walls were photographs, framed in wood and in silver. Most were old, black and white. Most were of the same couple; most were of her, I recognized. In all she was smiling, often on the arm of a serious looking man. In many she was looking at him with affection — her young, delicate, teasing features. In a few it was clear she had coaxed a smile from him, led him to something carefree — freed his thoughts — brought him into the present.

As I looked at their faces I was aware that I was looking into their past as they, in turn, looked forward into the future. What would it be like, in your youth of promise, to see ahead to your future self, alone, looking back at you along the long path? This was her ritual. A constant circuit of things — to try and maintain the connection to people — to repeat the litany of remembrance — ignorant that all life is an exercise in forgetting. No matter how we try, we cannot hold those who have left. We cannot reconstruct them from the fragments.

A telephone was on the side table. I placed my cup down, sat on the edge of the bed and dialled Beth's number. She answered with a cautious "hello."

"It's me."

"I didn't recognize the number. Where are you?"

"A friend's."

"I haven't heard from you in days. Where have you been? I've been worried —"

"Yes, I'm sorry. A friend just — listen. Tomorrow. Can we meet? Lunch? A drink?"

"Sure. I guess."

"I just think — you're right, that's all. I'd like to move forward. I'd like to make plans. Look, I'll call you tomorrow morning. I love you."

I lingered on the line after she'd hung up, then returned the phone to the table. I made the bed, with tight corners as my mother had taught me, then picked up the torn nightdress and my cup, retreated to the kitchen. I placed the nightdress in the garbage bag under the sink, taking out the bag and tying it securely. I cleaned up the evidence of my tea ritual, rinsing the cup and saucer in the sink, looking out the window into the dark.

I moved to the living room cabinet, selected another china cup and saucer, and placed them on the table at her place. The silver spoon I returned to the table in its sentinel position. Then, as an afterthought, I took three more cups and saucers, all mismatched, and set the table for four.

The thistle cup I pocketed.

I turned out the lights, closed the door. I locked the bolt and returned the key to the flower pot, dropped the garbage bag down the chute in the hallway.

Back in my own apartment, I placed the thistle cup and saucer on my desk. I moved again to the window and looked back to the dark space where she had been. Suddenly, I was tired. I was about to turn away, when I thought I saw, a floor up from hers, the shadowed movement of a curtain in the window.

ON THE STREET WHERE YOU LIVE

The body was there in the morning, when I looked out onto the street, as is my custom, a mug of coffee in hand, as I assess the day and plan my route. The sweep of light from the morning sun was unlikely to find the shadow that held him, the shadow that had caused me to doubt at first what I saw.

He was crumpled in the far curb a few buildings up, toward the intersection with Proskauer Street, in front of the small shop that sold confectionaries. Bäckerei Balzer, the sign said, the window display of pastries and tarts, cakes with sweet birthday greetings.

I didn't know if he was shot there — I assumed shot — or if he'd been dumped during the night. I vaguely recalled awakening in the dark hours, aware of a low rumbling — the sound of a truck, I told myself, adding meaning only now. I could see that there was little blood, although it had rained during the night. The rumbling may have been thunder. The rain may have washed the blood into the gutter — the half-moon gutter grate I now noticed beneath his head, like a rusted halo.

It was still early, and I watched as the few people on the street made a point of not noticing him, how they became suddenly keen on items in the shop windows or finding reasons to cross the street to some point of feigned interest or purpose — more energy invested in avoiding him than it would have taken to deal with it somehow. But maybe not. Who do you notify now? Since the war was lost — even before then, when order began crumbling — asking for help was viewed as weakness or complicity: complicity in his deed or the deed that took him. But by then my coffee was cold, and I released the curtain and turned back to my room. I wondered briefly of the impact on the confectioner's shop — the decline in business — particularly if the day proved to be as hot as the intensity of the low sun suggested it would be. A final day of summer, perhaps, stolen from the litany of fall.

Around noon I was ready to leave my apartment. This was the best time, just before lunch. Those who were out would not yet have returned for their noon meal; those inside would still be preparing it. I pushed my pamphlets into the canvas knapsack and opened my door an inch or so. The hallway was empty.

I stepped out, clicked my door shut. The single fixture overhead cast uneven light, so many dead flies in the bottom of its yellowed glass that I wondered why it didn't cast a speckled shadow on the carpet.

I pushed open the fire door to the stairs just enough to look, then moved quickly out of the hallway. The air in the stairwell was cool and musty, and the surroundings gave the sensation that I'd been transported back in time. Although the hallway was old — the carpet worn and in need of replacement, and the paint and wood trim speaking of a distant sensibility — in the stairwell it was brick and slabs of stone for footfalls, a smoothed groove worn by the traffic of years. The periodic need to update the glamour of the hallways, although now several decades behind, had once been a necessity. Here, though, behind the heavy door, all was as it had been at the start. Utilitarian. Who, in an emergency, would note the decor? Who, in a state of normalcy, would take the stairs over the elevator? Only a madman. Or someone with something to hide. Or me, I suppose.

In the lobby, the gilt was more faded. I pushed open the art deco door. The cut glass, although smeared grey and with the red remnants of a painted slogan, was still unbroken, and I grieved the declining level of vandals and mobs that can no longer be bothered to deface and damage such an obvious target. Where is the honour among thieves, the hierarchy? Now broken glass is just broken glass. Gone is the appreciation for destruction of the finer things, back when anarchy was more seldom, more selective — more a cry for help and less a broader frustration.

In the street the sun had been overrun by clouds, and the wind cut me — withdrew the earlier promise of warmth and pushed my face in his direction. I could have avoided the area easily — a half-block detour to the right, past the trolley stop. I wouldn't even have to cross the main boulevard. But I chose to go to the left, toward him, but keeping to the far side of the street.

Once I was opposite him, I slowed. He was young. His blond hair was matted with black blood, at the back, where the bullet had entered. A single wound. A trademark. The economy of the times.

I crossed the street, looking both ways, despite the lack of traffic. Stopped on the curb.

His head was turned, broken wire glasses twisted, half in place over his right eye, the left side turned upward onto his forehead as if in surprise. His eyes were open, searching the cobblestones for direction or meaning. There was blood on his right hand, a crusting at the second joint where his third finger was missing. Probably the easiest way to remove a ring as payment or souvenir. He wasn't in uniform — a simple jacket, heavy, suited for the late fall — scuffed leather shoes, wool pants, a dull shirt and tie. No hat, which I thought strange. Most men wear hats — the soft kind that can be shaped to their character. Mine was tilted and low on my brow, the front swept downward — to shade and suggest purpose.

Was he targeted? Did he figure on some list? We had not yet achieved the tolerance the new order promised, we'd just found new targets. Tolerance is temporary; targets are forever.

I checked my watch, afraid I'd lingered too long — missed my tram — made myself noticeable as the street traffic increased. Above me, in a third-floor room, I thought I saw a curtain move. No. The glint was likely the sun breaking free, shifting between buildings, reflecting off the glass. I pulled my collar up against the cold and turned to continue on my way — then turned back, as an afterthought, crouched, pulled the glasses from his face, stuffing them into my pocket as I hurried on through the shadows to the corner.

It was after six when I returned, my knapsack almost empty. I came home from a different direction, having seen a patrol vehicle through the broken window of the trolley and anticipated the patrol's route along the main streets. I stashed the last of my pamphlets under the seat, stayed on for two extra stops, and walked back through the side streets, past the rubble of the ruined buildings. Why be convenient for them? Why make their jobs too easy?

I entered my building through the side door off the alley — taking the back stairs to my floor. In my rooms, the curtains were shut against my urge to look. I placed the glasses on the mantel next to a broken picture frame and a brass candlestick. They sat at a comical angle, the cheap wire twisted — one of the circular lenses intact, the other broken in a sunburst just off centre. The blow had come from the lower left from his perspective.

I busied myself heating leftover soup on the gas burner, tore some black bread for my supper, allowed myself a swallow of wine from the open bottle, only occasionally looking up to his stare from the mantel.

That night, my fragmented dreams were full of anxious pursuit — someone ahead of me eluding my sight, someone behind. Echoed sounds. I woke anxious, sticky hot, thirsty.

I stumbled to my small kitchen. Poured some wine into a tumbler. Moved back to the sitting room, to the mantel, and picked up the glasses. I switched on the single lamp, turned the glasses until one lens produced a bright point of the light, the other a random scatter of lines. At the window, I pulled back the curtain an inch or so. The dark seemed complete, the moon's reflection staring at me from the window opposite. As my eyes adjusted, details emerged. Brickwork walls. Wires. Poles. The texture of the wet pavement. The heavy air holding the smoke down so it gripped the chimneys like fingers. As I looked out, I balanced the glasses on the index finger of my right hand, found the point of equilibrium, felt them gently sway.

He was still there. His position was different, though. Now he was on his back, rotated so his head was near the building, his feet to the gutter. His jacket was in disarray, as if the pockets had been rifled. So thorough. So pointless. Nothing of value is ever left. His shoes were gone now. I regretted not taking them; regretted that they were too small. I could see the sock on his left foot half on, hanging like the ear of a beaten dog.

Again, there'd been rain, enough to create small silver pools intermittently in the stones of the road. I felt an anger — that no one could be bothered — that he could be left for so long without someone taking the time to move him — drag him away to wherever they take them to be disposed of. But my anger was balanced by the stillness of the scene — how alone he looked, discarded, rejected. I looked down at the useless glasses in my hand. So often we expect the pieces to be more than the whole, but sometimes when things are broken apart they are just broken. They have no separate meaning.

I released the curtain, finished my drink, put the glass down on a small table by the window. Through this downward glance, I saw my shoes sitting by the chair. I saw, on the leather, the half-dozen flecks of dark brown, none larger than a letter in a book. I must have stood too close. The rain must have splashed some to the sidewalk where I'd stood — had made the sidewalk complicit in the act and now, by association, me. I touched my finger to my tongue, reached down with that finger and took one of the blood flecks on the tip. In the dim light it looked black against my grey skin. Its shape was irregular, with sharp edges. I moved my thumb against it and it fell through the darkness to the floor.

I grabbed my overcoat from the back of the chair and moved to the door. I took a surplus blanket from the closet and wrapped it over my shoulders, moved out into the dark hallway, gently closed my door just to the point that the latch began to engage. I opened the stairwell door carefully, eased it shut behind me — the hinges a muffled protest — then moved swiftly down in the cushioned steps of my slippers.

I stayed close to the buildings, in the shadows, avoiding the light of the one unbroken street lamp, crossing the street only when I was opposite him. His short hair was tipped with night frost. There was a scratch on his forehead where the wire frame of the glasses had cut in. I reached forward from the shadows, and he watched me close his eyes — gently, as I'd seen it done, feeling a guilt that I had not done this for him earlier. I considered returning the glasses, but they would only be taken by someone else. I straightened his legs, putting his feet together, adjusted his tie and jacket into position, smoothed his hair into a semblance of order with a sweep of my hand.

When I stood back up, the other man was there, watching us. Smaller than me. Dark hair under a cloth cap. An army great coat on his small frame, the service patch recently torn off, as evidenced by the loose threads at his shoulder. Boots new, laced with knotted string. There was a bruise on the side of his face, by his left eye: purple, slightly swollen, fresh. Otherwise his face was sunken, the hollowness emphasized by the shadows.

We said nothing. His breath leaked from between his lips as steady steam. I moved my right hand slowly, keeping his gaze, 'til it rested over my right pocket. I patted the pocket twice, hinting at possession of something he did not know I did not have.

A long second passed, then he stepped backward, left arm out, until his hand reached the brick wall. Another second, then he turned quickly, up the sidewalk to the corner, to the right into the dark. I watched until a distant church bell struck the hour, before I turned back to my charge.

I took the blanket from my shoulders and laid it over him, covered his face, crossed his arms to anchor it. The blanket, too, would be gone before the light, and I felt the chill of futility.

I looked down at him. At my feet, he stretched out from me like a shadow, a distortion of the light. I inhaled the sting of night air, searching for words or a sound to acknowledge him, this stranger. But the only sound was hurried steps on the wet pavement, echoing on the brick. I turned, expecting to be caught out again. But there was nothing. The steps faded into the night.

A movement caught my eye. His hat — weeds and trash hiding it, pinning it in a puddle by the alley. Wet, stained dark, it twitched in the wind like a dying thing.

The Ascent of Hank

During the time of which I speak, the world was a different place: status based; right and wrong; the shirts white, the jackets black, the ties a thin line of demarcation; dresses no more curious than the knee, a protective layer of slip to counter x-ray glasses, legs crossed; television monochromatic during the day, winking during the night, a test pattern in the wee hours when things really happened. Sensibilities were dealt with by emotional suppression, both internal and external, a double click of shot glasses rather than a mouse.

It was not a time of innocence itself, but rather a time of imposed innocence wrapped around our truer selves, like a cloak of invisibility.

But what of the people in particular.

Hank was an imposing figure who seemed most comfortable in a continuous slouch. He wasn't fat, just generously fleshed throughout his six-foot-five frame, resulting in a cumulative impression that his whole must greatly exceed the sum of his parts. His face was round and red, topped with intermittent tufts of short cropped black hair. His earlobes were large and dangly, leaving the less amply endowed with the impression that they must be uncomfortably weighty or catch the wind awkwardly.

His official title was Supply Procurement Officer, a bottleneck position: securing, storing, and finally distributing, to the high and lowly, everything from paperclips to electric typewriters.

Twenty-five years on the job had taught him nothing if not the wastefulness of the upper levels, his corporate betters — their cavalier and entitled and unbridled approach to supply consumption — of the consumption of *his* supplies. The supplies he ensured were always on hand in order to respond to their needs, their whims.

Sure, they may have had the education and the high paying jobs and the old school connections and the country clubs, the key to which required a nod and a wink and the special handshake and the glint of silver spoon. It wasn't that he even golfed — a game for the sweatered elite and the firstborn sons of corporate barons — he'd just like to be asked sometime.

But he held a different key. His control was of a more pedestrian nature. In his basement bunker row upon row of cardboard boxes, stacked like barricades, spoke of his initiatives to provide sober second thought to their extravagant office requests and to make sure plenty was put aside for a rainy day. Noah was less prepared.

Beads of condensation clung to the concrete wall as it sweat in the heat of the furnace, and the paint bled a stagnant odour of dampness from its blistered surface. The sunlight flowed with a corroded amber tinge through the single, grimy window high up near the ceiling, and distorted shadows swept by from the pavement beyond the cracked glass.

Hank's basement office was his kingdom. No little 'execu-jerk' ever risked dirtying his Florsheim leather shoes to venture down to screw up Hank's day by challenging his obstructive counter enquiries to their requisitions (*Requests for Order Clarification*, the *re*: portion of his memoranda read). Here he was free. He had his own coffee pot. A vending machine outside his door dispensed all manner of antique snacks. There was even a surplus army cot in the corner for when he felt there was no real need to return to his bachelor apartment — when the weather was too cold or too hot, or too wet or too dry to make the long bus ride bearable.

"Upstairs you've got no privacy," he liked to expound to the rapidly depleting list of anyone who'd listen. "You have to spend the day smiling and bowing and kissing the ass of them overpaid, college-graduate, French-press coffee drinking MBAssholes. Here I'm my own boss. I get the job done and I collect my two bits at the end of the day, thank you very much."

And that all made sense. The corporate order thrived, in a primordial ooze sort of way. Balance was maintained. Everyone was happy.

Until one day in June.

Hank pushed back his chair. It squealed on the floor — wooden fingers on a concrete blackboard. He looked again at the memo — a standard requisition form (an A13-27-R6/76, if you will) — rereading it aloud to confirm its ludicrous content:

Boxes, paper, plain white, 96 brilliance, 20 lb, 500 sheets per package; file folders, legal size . . . it went, on and on, carbon copy by carbon copy. He shook his head.

"They think it's a damn giveaway. Like it grows on trees or something."

He reached for the phone. No. This was too much. This required the personal touch.

The smudged carbon of the requisition in his hand, he dragged his feet across the floor as he moved to the service elevator with all the deadened enthusiasm of an old man facing the noose or a young man facing the aisle.

"Fuck you," he cursed as he spat at a silverfish scurrying off in pursuit of a new stench. He tried to duck under the low-hanging hot water pipes, but he clipped his head on the last of the three. It hissed at him, and he countered its curse with a long, drawn out "sssssssssshhhhhhhhhhhiiiiiiiit" as he rubbed his slightly scalded bald spot.

"For two fucking cents . . ." was his muttered invocation as he pulled open the cage door of the freight elevator. The inner doors opened — half up, half down — like the jaws of a giant metal whale, and he entered in. He pulled the bars of the outer door back across and gazed once more at his dark kingdom as the inner doors resumed their grim expression, then he spat into the crusted dirt at his feet.

The rising coffin whirred and clicked ominously. Hank glanced over to the framed inspection notice on the wall and amused himself trying to remember who was prime minister when the machine was last serviced. The rapid ascent caused his stomach to feel uneasy as it pushed downward, longing for the stability of his basement lair. He was moving into their world now, onto their turf. The rules were different up here. Watch your ass. Keep your enemies close, your friends closer — as a human shield against those close enemies.

On the thirty-fifth floor, Hank slammed his palm against the red stop button. The elevator lurched the final foot of its climb and the doors opened with a kind of screeching metallic belch.

Instinctively, Hank wiped his hands on his pants, shuffled his feet on the filthy floor mat, drew a palm of spit over his insubordinate cowlick. With a deep breath, he stepped out into the stinging cleanliness of the corporate world. The sun blinded him momentarily as it glinted off the chemically purified water in the cooler. The hum of the ventilation system dulled his senses. And in the air there was that odd smell of artificiality like — what was it — the sea? Spice?

"Hello, Hank."

"Huh?"

It was Benson, a minor vice-president, obliged to exchange pleasantries with the underlings, as current articles on employee morale required. So it had been written, so would it be done.

"Beautiful weather we're having, isn't it?"

"Uh, sure," Hank answered, as if he'd noticed, as if he'd even seen the outdoors in the last fortnight.

"Plans for the weekend?"

"Plans? No. No plans."

"Well, hopefully this warm weather will hold, eh? Well. Nice we could have this little chat." Here Benson smiled, or rather the thin slit that was his mouth elongated, which in Benson passed for a smile.

"Whatever," Hank replied to the already vanishing figure. *Just to the end of the hall*, he reminded himself. *I just gotta make it to the end of the hall.*

Hank shuffled on, his sliding steps drawing the static electricity from the carpet, and, like a condemned man with shaved head and split pant legs waiting for the switch to be pulled, he clenched his teeth for the static shock to come as he reached for the metal knob of the office door.

Brador Sarcawski, District Manager — Sales Division was formed into the artificial wood grain of the raised plastic insert. He took another deep breath and cleared his throat to adjust to his 'upper office voice' — a proper balance between righteous indignation and deference to imposed authority. Then entered he in.

"Mrs. Crutchen, Mr. Sarcawski has got to understand once and for all that just because —"

He stopped, even though he had taken sufficient breath for a solid paragraph or more.

"I'm sorry. May I help you?" came the dulcet reply.

There, where he had expected to find wallowing in a herniated swivel chair the amalgamated corporate structure of Sarcawski's personal gorgon Mrs. Crutchen, he instead saw a lithe form, daintily cross-legged, caressed in cascading patterns of colour, smiling in a most charming fashion. Mrs. Crutchen never smiled, although her teeth were often visible.

"You're not Mrs. Crutchen."

Her enjoyment at his obvious redundancy elicited from her a bright laugh and a smile, which she held before replying. She assumed, quite logically, that Hank's open mouth signalled he was not yet finished. He was, quite accurately, very finished indeed.

"Mrs. Crutchen is out sick. I'm Suzie. Suzie Lawrence. I'm filling in temporarily. Is there something I can do for you?"

He hadn't heard a thing. All he could do was notice how her voice danced through the words like music. He wasn't sure what kind of music, but he was pretty sure it was from one of those funny instruments the ancient Greeks were always strumming. She had offered her hand, but he could only make a sort of bow in its direction, unworthy to make direct contact.

"Are you all right . . ." she asked, withdrawing her hand. She noticed the name tag pinned at an awkward angle on his lapel. ". . . Hank?"

So caring, he thought. He thrust out his own hand and presented her with the requisition form, biting his lip like a schoolboy delivering a Valentine.

"Oh yes. This is the requisition form I typed for Mr. Sarcawski. My initials are there in the corner. Is there something wrong with it? Did I make a mistake?"

"Oh no! You could never — I mean, you . . . uh . . . you never . . ." he gasped, unable to remember why the paper had offended him so, or why her perfume reminded him of spring, or how to breathe. ". . . you . . . never said what size of paper you need. I didn't want to send up any old stuff and make you go to all the trouble of having to send it back down because I'd gone and sent you the wrong size."

"Why that's very considerate of you. Thank you. Yes, size is important. Standard eight-and-a-half by eleven will do — or do you require it in metric?"

"No, no, no, no, no, no, no, no . . ." he trailed off.

"Here, let me correct that."

She tugged the form from his grip, and added the change, using a standard company-issue Bic Cristal. *Medium blue, like her eyes*, he thought.

"Shall I initial the revision?" she asked, but she was already doing so. "I'll certainly try and be more careful on the next order. I can't imagine what trouble I've put you through, coming all the way up here from —?"

"— the basement . . ."

She followed his downward gaze and intense fascination in the carpet at his feet. "And in your best shoes," she added, with another small laugh that buoyed his gaze back up to her. She handed back the form and the pen.

"No. No trouble. Don't mention it. Mistakes happen. Glad I could help. We're all on the same team after all, right?

"Right."

"Right. Well. I can see you're busy — important stuff — I'll just leave you . . . to . . . it." And with that he backed from the office, resisting the urge to nod his head and tug his forelock.

Outside, Hank leaned his head against the pleasant coolness of the closed door, then pivoted on his heels with a youthful agility and began to whistle his way down the hall.

"Mornin' again, Mr. Benson."

"Pardon?" Benson countered, caught off guard with a stenographer.

"You were right: kind of day that makes you glad you're alive."

"Quite."

In the freight elevator, Hank compressed his lips in an expression that on others would have denoted glee, licked his finger, and drew a heart in the dirt on the floor.

The elevator seemed to float downward on a breath, and the doors opened with a sigh. He stepped out from the cage doors into his basement world of diamond-sparkled walls and inhaled deeply of the moist air.

"Like the sea," he thought. "Vast, like the sea."

He rattled his head off all three of the hot water pipes, but just laughed at the sweetly melodic tones the impacts made. He sat down upon his throne of cracked wood, placed the crystal pen in the centre of his inbox, and carefully opened his love poem — the initialled requisition. And in a voice touched for once with tenderness and affection, he began to read to his six-legged friends the secrets of true romance:

"Boxes, paper, plain white, 96 brilliance, 20 lb, 500 sheets per package; file folders, legal size . . ." his voice echoing as in a cathedral, filtering up to the outside world through the stained glass window.

RAG PICKERS

The event was advertised as black-tie, which I hate. The idea of
gowns and ruffles was enough to send me screaming. I was never
one of those little girls in pinks and crinoline, her hair in French
braids, perfecting her twirls *en pointe* until blood collected in her
toe shoes. I was the one in blue jeans, my hair in a straight ponytail,
challenging the boys for supremacy on the monkey bars.

But then I thought, *Black tie. Why not?* So I went down to this
little secondhand clothes place just off of downtown. *Rag Pickers*,
it was called. Just a shabby store that lived in the shadow of the
fashionable shops: one of those buildings with the narrow front,
and peeling paint on a heavy wooden door, and row upon row of
other people's discards — with a small sideline in sex toys and vinyl
corsets.

There had to have been five hundred men's suits marching in
tight formation in several rows, iterating the narrow space between
shades of brown and grey. But I tried on this old tuxedo jacket —
heavy and well made, double breasted and tailored in that fifties
style. Pants to match. Satin stripe along the trouser leg. Black vest
with satin trim. Patent-leather, straight-lace shoes. A black bowtie
and a long silk scarf in pale blue to match my eyes. Perfect.

God, I looked good — if the cracked funhouse mirror they had
was any judge. Best forty dollars I ever spent. My hair was shorter
then and swept up on one side, in a kind of Myrna Loy style from
the *Thin Man* movies, or Mary Astor, from *The Maltese Falcon* —
like I'd seen on the old movie channel — the movies I love to curl
up and watch on rainy noir Saturday nights. But I had something
they never had: these amazing streaks of cobalt blue and vermilion
red screaming up from my scalp.

This was back when I was poor. No. Not poor. Just living well
on an income below the poverty line, in a one-bedroom third-floor
walk-up I shared with an ample cross section of God's multilegged
creatures — an apartment spotted with castoff furniture I'd picked
up like strays on the curbside.

On the night, Vince arrived to pick me up — let himself in with
his key. Vince was his stocky self, in a rented tuxedo that fit him like

a tarp for a smart car bungeed over an SUV. Almost thirty-five, and no tuxedo of his own? The world is in decline, my father would have said. But he does not like suits, our Vince. His office of financial advisers is all dockers and golf-shirts, like they all invested the wardrobe account on a casual Friday. Vince is more for announcing your success through toys: a flashy car, a downtown condo, the all-inclusive golf weekend with the lads. So when I burst from my bathroom with a "ta-da" and a triple spin, all I got was a stare.

"Well?"

"You look —"

"Fabulous?"

"— like a guy."

"Sure, but like a fabulous guy!"

And I was fabulous. And the evening was fabulous. How a nineteen-year-old copy editor at a tiny regional press got invited to a major fundraiser for the symphony probably speaks to the overall bankruptcy of the arts, but what the hell. There was a live band playing jazz, a sprinkling of funky people, good food served in tiny portions on silver trays by staff who probably make twice my take-home — oh, and domestic champagne fizzing in tall skinny glasses.

And the dancing! Our Vince isn't much for dancing. But Louise is, and we made quite the couple 'cuttin' a rug' — me in my tuxedo; Louise in her mint green bridesmaid dress with the balloon sleeves and the feathered fascinator sweeping back like a peacock's tail from her short-cropped platinum hair. And Jeremy was there, too: thin, tall and dashing in a tailored grey pinstripe with pale pastel accessories and a rhinestone stickpin through his silk tie so large you could have used it for a walking stick. Man, he can dance! Jitterbug. Jive. You name it. And he's gay, so Vince doesn't mind too much him spinning and dipping me. But Vince got the slow dance at the end of the night, his feet keeping a heavy beat, his hands drifting like high school had never ended.

It was a blast — that is until we got home and Vince, pissed and horsing around, ripped one of the pockets of my jacket trying to get me into bed. Not a whole lot of romance in our Vince. To him foreplay is best limited to the time it takes for the bodies to freefall to the mattress. Torn clothes, well, that was a bonus to him — a little rough-and-tumble for the same price.

Later on, he left to go back to his apartment — I'd kicked him in the ribs enough for snoring that he finally staggered out the door. Who am I kidding? He was happy to go. Not for our Vince a warm slumber of woven limbs. Not for him a lazy morning spent in bed with lumpy instant coffee and powdered whitener and the crossword puzzle — unless he knew a stand-up fuck in the shower was on the short-term agenda. With his slam of the door I'd shrugged off the thin covering of sleep. Vince can fall asleep after sex — during, if the truth be told. For him, it's an act, not an emotion. For me, sex always leads to something else — something less restful — something more like disquiet.

I rolled over and saw the pile of my clothes on the hardwood floor, like remains awaiting identification. I saw the jacket rumpled and inside out, with the tear like a thin-lipped smile. I stretched a bare arm out from under the sheets into the cold and snagged the jacket, pulling it up onto the bed to see how badly torn it was — if I could repair the damage Vince had done.

Not too bad. It was the inside pocket mainly, the shiny fabric torn along a partial seam that looked as if it'd been repaired before, the tear the width of a hand. But as I pulled and pressed the fabric in place I could hear, feel really, the crinkle of something in the lining. So I slipped my hand inside the opening, slowly into the mouth of the tear, and removed a single folded piece of paper.

A note.

It was dark in the room, the morning still too young to reach past the curtain. I didn't want the shock and glare of the lamp, so I slid out of bed, jacket in hand, and moved over to the window where the glow from the streetlight was enough to read by.

The paper was nice — you know: thick, the edges soft and rolled, like frayed cloth. The ink had that look you get from a fountain pen — that slight variation in weight and colour. It was a woman's hand, like I remembered of my grandmother's — the writing the swoop and curls of another age.

I wish you were dead, it read.

Now that's something to find in your dark apartment, at three in the morning, by the light of the street lamp. No date. No signature. Whoever wrote it must have figured — figured what, since it had been sewn into the lining of the coat? Figured that whoever would find it would know, or that it would never be found? That it would sit undiscovered?

I imagined a distant couple — the obligatory hug — the feigned affection, her hand seeking the hidden message through the fabric, the focused pressure while it worked its real magic — finding its way to the wearer's heart, making them twitch with unease.

I sat down in the chair by the window — the oversized chair where I sit wrapped in an old blanket from childhood to watch my late-night movies — covered myself against the dark and the cold, then fell asleep, the paper and jacket held close to my face. I only woke when the phone rang around noon — when Vince phoned wanting — what? Writing this I can't even remember what Vince wanted. I can only remember the sound of the ringing, the note on the hardwood floor, partially caught in a rectangle of light through the window, the light bringing out the cream of the paper and the aged patina of the wood, while everything outside its reach was grey.

That afternoon I went back to the store with the jacket in hand. The sign in the window said they did repairs, and they had a little tailor shop in the back. As the lady was looking the damage over, I asked, casually, where the jacket came from.

"An estate sale," she said. "It came in with a bundle of other things: dresses, pants — last week or the week before. Some furs, too, but they take a while to clean properly."

"Any more jackets," I asked?

"I can fix this — it's okay."

"No. I'd like to see if there are any others."

"Look around you. There're jackets everywhere."

"From that supply."

"Oh. That lot? Yes. A few, I guess."

"Where? Which rack?"

"How would I know? Do you know how many bags of clothes we get in here in a month? We don't keep them separate. We hang the suits with the suits, the dresses with the dresses. You get our system? It's not rocket science."

"And you clean them?" I asked, as a thought occurred to me.

The hesitation before her definitive "of course" was enough. In order for the letter to have survived this long, the jacket couldn't have been drycleaned much since the note had first been placed within the lining. Or maybe the lining protected it. I grabbed the jacket back.

"Hey! Don't you want me to repair the seam?"

But with a backward wave I was gone from the store.

Back home I sat in the armchair by the window, the standing lamp behind me on high. I held the jacket close to my glasses and went over each square inch with the precision of a CSI veteran. What I expected to find, I'm not sure. A stain, maybe, or a mark. Something that would give me a hint as to the jacket's past life — to the context of the message I'd found.

Vince would have said I was crazy, obsessive. He would have mocked me for trying to figure it out. We'd have gotten into a fight about it. I'd have tried to laugh it all off, but he wouldn't have let it go, stockpiling his certainties like stones. He'd have to win. Which is why I'd stopped telling him stuff like this. Or maybe I never had to begin with. It's not what we're about, Vince and me.

We're using each other. He gets someone young and edgy to show he's still got it — slumming for sex. I get maturity, or what passes for it — a ticket into another world every other weekend, where tabs get paid and credit cards get honoured. Oh, and sex, if I'm to be fully truthful.

Up close the jacket smelt faintly of tobacco. Not cigarettes, but something more aromatic, I imagined — earthier, like cigars — or a pipe. Does anyone still smoke a pipe? Ironically, maybe. I could imagine Jeremy with a meerschaum pipe, pontificating on the declining status of arts in Canada, holding it by the bowl as he stabbed the stem in the air for emphasis.

I remembered the cigar I'd enjoyed with the girls after Cindy's wedding — the fancy ones Eve had smuggled back from her Cuban vacation. We'd all coughed and sputtered, washed the smoke down with red wine and laughter. And I had remembered then, wiping the water from my eyes, the smell of my father's pipe smoke on his jackets, or the vests he always wore — how his things had held that smoky smell years after he'd gone, like if I opened a book of his poetry that had sat in the blue smoke of his room.

There was also a small burn mark, no larger than the head of a match, at the left cuff, and on the lapel a reddish-brown mark, like paint or old blood, the size of a fingernail — not on top of the fabric, but worked into the threads — a mark I now saw as lipstick.

And I imagined a second life for the jacket — a life after the note, as if a head had rested on that lapel in comfort — being comforted. Tears dried, perhaps, after the lipstick had already been smeared by a rough kiss.

Not my kiss. I so seldom wear lipstick any more, and certainly not on the night I'd worn the jacket. Vince didn't like it — the feel of it — even though we didn't kiss much, not romantically. And our Vince was not one to smoke a cigar, or to embrace me for the time needed to transfer the nostalgic scent to my clothes.

I wish you were dead.

I didn't wish Vince dead. At least not in the purely biological context. But I looked around my small room — at the garage-sale chic I surrounded myself with: a small wooden wardrobe, doors missing, overflowing with shapeless jackets and men's shirts; unframed art bought from guys on the street corner; secondhand books piled by my bed, those I'd already read acting as my night table. All things that defined me. Things he'd always laughed at without humour.

I folded the note carefully and placed it back in the lining. Then I took out the needle and thread I so seldom used — the repair kit in the little leather case — the gift my father had given me when I quit school and moved out. Part of the various emergency kits he'd given me over the years "so a young lady can be independent," as if having a hammer and screwdriver, or a sewing kit, or a winter blanket and chocolate for a car I'd never own could keep a girl from finding the wrong man for the wrong reasons.

I wish you were dead.

Now my father was dead, and there was no one to try to protect me from the world by showing me how to do things, how to rely on myself. There was no one for me to push back hard against to gain momentum in the direction I'd chosen.

I concentrated, threaded the needle in only four tries, and put the seam back in place —smoothed the material — sealed the note up once more. Then I put the jacket in a shopping bag.

"Tomorrow I'll go to the Goodwill bin by the Safeway parking lot," I told myself. And I went. Tossed the bag in. Passed on the letter to the next recipient. Trusted in fate that it would find someone who needed it.

I kept the vest, though. I wear it on occasion, at the theatre or open-mic readings, or alone in my apartment sitting by the window, watching my movies, drinking sparkling wine from a garage-sale tumbler.

LAST WORDS

Maria told me, the night before I left: "The last lesson our parents teach us is mortality." But her lesson did not include how to deal with becoming an orphan in late middle age.

I sit cross-legged on the hardwood floor in my father's den, two walls of books rising floor to ceiling in front of me. Against the far wall is the desk the old man built: solid, two columns of wooden drawers in oak, a two-inch thick top of some sort of wood covered over in a black leather. Ornate was never his style. Function over form.

Behind the desk rests a swivel chair, but I have chosen the floor. I've sat in that chair — his chair — hundreds of times before, but not since. Now it seemed presumptuous. Too heavy a metaphor to take on just yet. Besides, I have packing to do. A task to hold my focus.

On the floor are several dusty cardboard boxes. Each box is taped shut; none are labelled. Some have water stains on the sides, or their corners are dented. Stacked next to them are new boxes, flattened, waiting to be assembled and filled with the books that laden the shelves.

Maria had told me not to do this — to leave the packing to my sister. But I knew Maggie would just toss in the first books she could grab until a few token boxes were full, then explain that the rest had been donated to charity: the homeless, the distant, the needy yearning for literature, or the biography of a long-dead world leader, or the poetry of a longer-dead romantic. I don't know why, but I couldn't allow it to be like that.

So I rented a van and drove two days to get here. We don't have the money — Maria was right — but she put up only token resistance, finally turning away — walking back down the hallway to the kitchen, my last words of persuasion lost in the dark, falling to the carpet at her heels without ever reaching her.

So many books.

My family moved into this house when I was five. A simple two story, but my father had the builder add the den: a small room at the back of the house, away from the busyness of the kitchen or the TV in the family room, with the bedrooms all upstairs. Its window overlooks the small garden, bright with early morning light. Whether he intended it as the suburban equivalent of a manor house library I don't know. Perhaps it was just his small show to the world, or to himself.

I know what the old boxes contain. Letters. Speeches. Reports that my father wrote during his days as an engineer with the government. Flood protection. Watershed management. Bridge reconstruction. Inspections of facilities during the spring: to ensure public safety, to establish plans and set them in action. And awards. Framed acknowledgements. Forty-plus years of service. He boxed it all up himself when he retired. Put them in the back of the den closet. Evidence of his existence. Too valuable to throw away; too distant to display.

On the open walls are pictures he painted. When he travelled for work he'd stop to take photographs of things that interested him. Buildings, mostly. Or farm scenes. Old barns sinking into the prairie under the weight of the years.

The composition is even and balanced, depicting an ordered world in collapse. Like the man himself. Sinking under his own weight, factors he had not anticipated in his planning, in his calculations.

But he was a good painter. A good eye for detail and perspective. Not good enough for acknowledgment, though. And I wonder if he knew — if that gnawed at him at all — or whether he just turned to his art for an escape and asked nothing more of it.

The den was where he smoked his cigars and lost himself in his books. The smell of tobacco like manhood itself as it had been taught to him.

The den was where I was called when I had strayed across the line, needed a man-to-man chat. The awkward 'you've reached that age' talk. The 'candle burning at both ends' talk. The 'you've disappointed your mother' talk — the worst of them all. I would stare at my feet as he built his solid ethical case, then look up at a wall of books when it was time to offer my thin answer, hoping that somehow words would spill out over the edges of some text to wash clean my sins. Sometimes they did, but they were never enough.

But I remember, at five, wandering into this room when he was out. He had left a book he'd been reading open on the desk. I picked it up, looking at these strange marks on the page, incomprehensible to my small mind — tears coming so easily, so suddenly. The childish frustration at being unable to make sense of these secrets that held his attention.

Then at twelve. Knocking. Asking for a book — asking to borrow from his shelves — ready to deny my own shelf of boy's adventures. I remember his thoughtful gaze. How he put down his own book; how he took the cigar from his mouth — the kind with the white snow owl on the box and on the band — placing it on the saucer of his coffee cup; how he ran a sure finger across a row until it rested on a leatherbound book. Short stories. I see the book now. My eye goes to it now without difficulty. I recall the sureness with which he handed it to me. No rules. Not a word between us. It was heavy for me, so light in his own grip. Then he took up his own book and his cigar and returned to his reading.

I remember opening the book when I was back in my room, upstairs. How it carried the smoke of his cigars on the pages — as if he had opened the book with me, as if he were there as I read, following along with me as I struggled to make sense of it, as I formed the longer words, spoke them in whispers so I could own them in some way.

The stories were old, of their time. A sea adventure, one. Another about a horse ride though a distant land. But another was about a man and a woman speaking across a table at a restaurant. Just that. So simple. I reread it when I'd finished the book, then again until I thought I could feel something happening — some movement beneath the simple surface that I could not put into categories — that unsettled the unmade bed of my childhood in a way I found pleasing.

And then, so many years later, I wrote my first book — built my own simple layers in stories, and presented it to him — the hardcover, with its shining dust cover. He took it from me as if I had brought something valuable from afar. He took a fresh cigar from the holder in his jacket pocket, chewed on the end as he examined the book. Weighed it in his right hand. Turned it over. Opened it, with that crack that new books have. He looked up from the title page. I hadn't signed it. He smiled because I hadn't signed it. A joke between us — how no one should ever presume to write in a book, not even the author. He reached for a match and lit his cigar, gave me a glance as he shook the match out that told me it was time to go — to leave him to his inspection of my work.

I returned to my room upstairs — a room I had not lived in for almost five years at the time. I lay on the floor, on my back, looking at the childhood toys on the shelf as my father read my book in the corner den a floor below — the long reach for acceptance.

And when Mother called us both to dinner several hours later, he was slow to arrive. He left the book in the den, said nothing of it, but touched my shoulder so lightly as he passed by to his chair at the head of the table, a slight smile on his face as he took his seat. He winked at Mother, as he always did — flirting with his wife of thirty years at the time. Said only: "Your boy is a writer." Then took a dinner roll and passed the bowl to me.

The book sat on the corner of his desk after he'd read it. Casually. So visitors would see it. So he could mention it in passing. And when I would visit, he'd ask me what I was working on, and at first I would offer the usual vague answers writers collect, shadows insufficient to the light. Until time collected more rapidly than my words on a page and I could offer nothing more. And then we spoke no more about it.

I suppose I felt the burden of being almost good enough. Of having talent enough to try and to hope, but not enough to succeed. For a while I taught writing — got the job during a time when one local book of moderate success was enough to teach at the local college. Then I gave even that up. Because no second book came. Because I tired of the students. Tired of them constantly asking were they talented? Was their writing special? How do they cash in? Tired of them disappearing at the end of each year, with more than a few of them quickly exceeding my own limited résumé, succeeding despite my guidance.

I don't mind it anymore. Better to be a minor talent and accept it. I quit trying to create my heartbreaking masterwork. I learned to leave my ambitions in the desk drawer. And over the long years I filled my time with small employments, jobs that paid the way and not much more.

And my book went on my father's shelf, among the others. No special place. It would have been wrong for it to have a special place. It went with the others, in its spot, according to the system he had, which was none, but which still allowed him to find anything he wanted when he wanted it with just a moment's contemplation.

And now I see him as he was in the final year, the tragedy of age — slowing, hesitant in thought, a mind shuffling. Nouns are the first casualties — somewhere, something, someone — the lack of certainty taking on an anxious priority to prove the ghost of a recollection real — reaching in his mind for the proof of a thought, but the paper crumbling to dust at the slightest touch.

I would talk to him, then, on my infrequent visits, coaxing him from his den to walk with me along the winding paths of the city in the slight chill of a fall day, pale sunlight making leafless silhouettes of the trees. I would use science and engineering to make him feel comfortable — pointing to the form of a steel bridge, the geometry of a stone arch, the movement of water knifing over a weir. I could see how he took comfort in the science, in the math, in the knowing, speaking to me freely of details he'd long known even though I was never sure he remembered my name.

And he still had his books. He could always escape into his books.

Mercifully it was the heart attack that took him so soon afterwards, so suddenly, as he returned to his den from the kitchen, coffee in hand. It dropped him to his knees in front of his chair, in front of his books — time only to place the cup down on the floor, the cigar to one side, the white owl perched on the saucer. He rested his head on the chair cushion, as if in prayer. Mother found him hours later — thinking he'd dropped something — lost something — his cold touch sinking her to her knees as well.

When I dream of him now — the dreams where we can't remember that the dead are dead — he is always as I remember him in this room. Soon I will be older than that, and the father in my dreams will be the younger man.

The light has shifted now. The shadows have moved across the wall and floor, swept the desk clean. I've wasted hours, accomplished little. I focus on the task at hand, fold the cardboard — fit tabs and slots — make a new box.

I decide to pack the books in order, to maintain his system. I move to the upper left shelf. Soon the box is full, but the change is hardly noticeable. A literary Sisyphus, the work endless, the shelf refilling itself no matter how many books I remove.

He's been dead for over five years now, and each time I'd visit Mother urged me to pack up the books, take them all with me, empty the room. But I couldn't. Always there was the need for his room to be there each time I returned. It being intact was as important as the way she greeted me at the door, offered tea, a slice of something sweet and familiar. But I would take one or two books each time, to keep her happy, transport them across the country to find a home in my own collection, within my own system.

But now she's been gone for six months. The house sold quickly. I knew this would happen. I told my sister this would happen. I told Maggie. But I never told her that I knew it was necessary. That it had to happen sooner, not later. She's in the arts, my sister — a theatre assistant, in need of the money just to survive. No, that's cruel of me. She's always been happy so far below the poverty line that if poverty were water she would long ago have ceased to flounder.

The shelves hold nothing of real value to a collector. Two-dollar yard-sale items at best. I'll never read more than a few. Maria was right: we have no room for them. They'll just sit in our basement. But each book, when opened, smells of tobacco smoke, and I run through a confused jumble of moments, feel my age collapse in on itself, and I think — I don't know — that maybe by keeping my father's library intact I can keep him intact.

I pull down another handful of books, and the remainder domino on the shelf. And there it is. My own book. I take it down. The dust jacket is torn. A younger self, faded, stares at me from the back cover. The book falls open with the ease of use.

I fan the pages and find, throughout, pencilled notes in the margins. The writing varies. Some is the sure style I recognize from his letters and reports. Some transitions to the small, cramped handwriting when he was older. Nearer the end. During the time of our walks.

He'd broken his own rule and written in it. Sometimes a phrase is underlined, with a simple *yes* in the margin. Or his comment connects to a larger thought, as if he were making a reply. Sometimes it showed that he understood the connection of the stories to my own life. Sometimes the marginalia spoke of doubt, of regret. *Did I really say that? Did I really leave you feeling that way? Where was I that you never told me this?* And in the back is repeated the phrase *my son wrote this*, over and over, in the awkward block letters of a child, filling the flyleaf, spilling to the edges.

He had reread the book. Returned to it, even at the last, Mother had told me. He read and reread the pages, long after he could no longer retain the meaning — he would sit, an unlit cigar in his mouth.

My father had often read aloud passages or phrases he liked. He felt you needed to read something aloud to truly own the words — especially poetry: "good men crying how bright the frail deeds might have danced," or death having no dominion, or laying of the gentle hand upon the faithless heart. And now I sat there and did the same. I read his words out loud, not caring if my sister should return and catch me — not knowing what I'd say — but only wanting for those brief moments to let his words hang in the air and feel him alive, feel him speaking to me as we had never spoken.

Now the room is empty. The boxes are set in inelegant, unengineered stacks by the front door. Without the weight of books, the room seems so small, as if the walls have drawn in. The light from the window, filtered through the dusty air, does nothing but wash the scene with age. The single chair and desk are square and utilitarian.

I move the boxes to the rental van for the long drive. I close the front door of the house and pocket the key to return to my sister.

Conversations with Cows

ACT ONE

"There you are."

Jordan continues down the steep slope of carefully mowed grass toward her — toward the bottom of the long yard and the fence of wooden posts and three-strand wire that delineates it from the pasture and scrub trees beyond. She doesn't acknowledge him — continues her focused stare at something distant he cannot see. He stops a few feet behind her and to one side. Looks around, as if waiting his turn.

Kate leans on a wooden post, in a posture both relaxed and tense, staring out past to — to what? He looks at her, at her hair oddly disarrayed — like always, but somehow more so — then out again to where she's looking — still nothing — then back at her. She has a can of beer in her left hand — one of those sour beers that she prefers and he hates. She turns the can slowly, the label design an explosion of bright colours, fragments of unidentifiable fruit. Her equally bright Hawaiian shirt catches what little breeze there is. At her flipflopped feet rests a large canvas bag. One hand, her right, is dappled in white paint. An oddly speckled rag sticks out from the back pocket of her fluorescent blue shorts.

"You're missing the party," he says, always more comfortable with the obvious. "I turned around, and you were gone. People were asking where you went."

Still nothing. He glances back toward the house, but it's too far beyond the rise to see, hidden by the manicured hedgerow.

"You should come back to the barbeque," he continues. "Back up to the house. Clark is cooking steaks! You can smell them." He turns his face to the sky, as if offering the world, but the world does not always deliver. "Or you could, if the wind was the right direction." And the wind offers nothing but dust and a hint of decay. He feels an uncomfortable familiarity with the moment, as if mired in unyielding mud while a fast-moving object travels on a collision course from a great distance.

"Come back," he tries again. "It's too hot to be standing down here out in the open."

The late summer sun is hot pressure on his face — the pricks of sweat pushing onto his skin, staining through his patterned, collared shirt. He presses his open can of beer against his forehead; faint sounds of distant country music rise in the air, adding to his discomfort. He carries a plastic bag with more cans of sour beer — an offering — but it cuts into his hand, so he lays the burden at his feet. He takes two more steps toward her, then stops as she starts to pick ineffectually at the paint on her hand.

"Mad dogs and accountants go out in the midday sun," she says, then tunelessly hums fragments of an unremembered song. "Who wrote it? Cole Porter? Noel Coward? Gershwin? Taylor Swift? It's hard to place it, what with the tinnitus of steel guitar cresting the grassy knoll. I thought the blues were bad, but listening to the twang of that country shit wafting up from that antebellum manor house they call an acreage makes you want to put your head in an oven, if only to muffle the sound."

He laughs, her sharp judgement a possible sign that all's well, decides to fuel the fire. "Their house? Is it big? I didn't notice." His tone is innocence intended to gain purchase on the slippery surface of her conversation.

"It has wings. They showed us wings! The north wing where the children have their bedrooms and playroom and their own TV room. The south wing, where the adults have their master bedroom and their separate home offices, and the gym and the post office and the town square and the helipad —"

"They do not have a heli —"

"What kind of person —" her eyes are bright now, a glow of energy around her intense enough to cast shadows, "— what kind of people would hire some clearly drug-addled landscape architect to drop this grand Alcázar haphazardly on ten acres — a newly planted orchard on one side, a newly dug lake on the other, a winding volcanic stone driveway you can see from space. And Clark's big, black truck. Big enough that it has its own postal code. *Look upon my works, ye mighty, and despair!*"

"What —"

"But back here —" she continues, without a breath "— down at the end of the landing-field manicured lawn, where the fertilizer and chemicals stop — we find the fence, built to keep nature out. Beyond lies pasture land and virgin forest — if any forest nowadays can still make that claim. Enjoy it while you can."

"Alcázar?"

"The castle. The chateau."

"You mean the house."

"Yes. The house."

"They piss you off because they're rich — or worse, because they don't know how to do rich properly?" She turns to him, a searching look in her eyes that unnerves him — drives him all the more to make her laugh. "Or is it the house itself, full of big, blank walls with no art on them — just framed hockey sweater after framed hockey sweater?"

She smiles despite herself. "The religious iconography of our time."

"Just come back up —" he motions.

"To the barbeque."

"Yes."

"For a steak."

"Sure."

"I'm vegan."

"Since when?"

"Since now."

"Convenient."

"I like to keep my morals flexible to suit the occasion."

He shakes his head, laughs, then looks back at her, gauging the direction the storm is coming from.

"You've been to the car. You've retrieved your bag of tricks." He nods toward the bag at her feet.

"Ah, you noticed." She moves her paint-speckled hand down to her side, but she doesn't fully block it from his view. "One point to you."

"You artists like to keep your morals close and your magic closer?"

"Just in case. That basilica of a family room might need a mural for the ceiling — something hockey themed. But I'm not an artist, am I? I'm an arts administrator."

He hears the hint of familiar hurt in her voice. "You're an artist," he reassures. "You have a BA and you work as an administrator for an arts organization. You run a festival. You write grant proposals." .

"And answer the phones, and beg the accounting firm next door for free use of their copier."

"But an artist first."

"Yes! An artist first! I am but a slave to my muse. And I like what I'm doing. I like encouraging art with nothing more than a handful of pennies." She sweeps an accusing finger up the hill — "But those idiots up there wouldn't know about that" — then back at him. "And I have *two* BAs."

"Hey, I have a degree, too."

"In commerce," she snorts. "You haven't read a book in years."

"No. But I've seen some spreadsheets that are clearly works of fiction."

Amused, she taps her index finger on his chest.

"You are a philistine!"

"I'm a —?"

"Look it up."

"I know what a philistine is. Look, just come back to the house. You don't have to have a steak. You could have —"

"— a salad? Ha! You'd never live down the Cro-Magnon shame of your fellow cave dwellers if I had a salad. I can hear them now," she continues, grunting the words. "*That not food; that what food eats.*"

"The guys aren't that bad."

"The guys? The boys? Da bros? You're ten years older than most of them. Puberty is still crying havoc in the limbic system of their brains. You should be guiding them to maturity, not climbing into the sandbox. Not being a willing participant in their tomfuckery."

"Tomfuckery?"

"You heard me."

Something is wrong. She's off script. More aggressive than usual. More cutting. He exhales forcefully, shakes his head as if to clear it, looks down at his feet as if to ground himself.

"You know I came to the oil business late. Hell, I've only been with the company three months. I have to get to know their world — get to know these people. I have to —"

"— earn your stripes? Your scars? Make the trains run on time?"

"That's not fair."

"We're not talking about fair."

"Oh, is that what we're *not* talking about. It's really hard to tell sometimes." He sighs, offers his hand, softens his tone. "Just come on back. Clark promised fireworks when it got dark."

"The promise all new brides are given. As much as I like a sky full of colour, no."

He withdraws his hand, deciding on the direct approach.

"You're being stubborn?"

"It's one of my charming idiosyncrasies."

"I know you don't like them —"

"Don't respect them —"

"Fine. Don't respect them."

"Or like them."

"But Clark is my boss —"

"— and a misogynist prick and an environmental rapist."

"— and Jocelyn —"

"— has so much plastic in her when she dies she'll be her own environmental disaster."

"Please!" His sudden explosion stops her short. "Don't do that."

"What?"

"Finish my sentences."

"Then stop being so fucking predictable."

"Whoa!" He puts up his hand. "Where did that come from?"

She freezes. Looks at him in a way unfamiliar to him. "I don't know. Nowhere. I'm . . ." She turns away, her voice suddenly small. "I'm sorry."

He takes a step toward her. Puts his hand on her shoulder. She reaches up, placing her hand on his. Her touch is light, unsubstantial, as if she were still not fully there with him, a mirage in the heat.

"It's okay," he says. "If it helps, I don't really like them either. But if you could just try to be nice to them —"

But she steps away, places her can of beer on the nearest fence post, then crouches beside her canvas bag on the ground. She rummages through it, taking out two small cans of paint, one black and one white, balancing them on a patch of rough earth, then retrieves a blister pack of nicotine gum from the bag. As she pops out the last piece and puts it in her mouth, she watches a bird — a hawk, he thinks, as he follows her line of sight — sitting on a power pole, turning its head to watch them as if considering, for a lazy moment of hubris, their potential as prey. She rises slowly, keeping the bird in sight, then looks at the empty pack in her hand. She stretches her arm out, the elbow bent like a falconer, the plastic pinched between her bent finger and thumb, a loaded gun.

"Don't do that," he says, firmly.

"What?"

"Don't drop trash on their —"

And she swings her forearm out, flicks the plastic to the ground a few metres from her feet. He sighs, bends to pick it up.

"It's rude."

"Rude?"

"Disrespectful. To them. Tossing trash."

"Disrespectful. Like them building this Taj Mahal to the greater glory of money way out here where nature can get a really good look at what it's sacrificing its existence for."

He holds out his right hand, the plastic in his palm.

"And this is different?"

"You're comparing that to what they've done?" She pushes her gum forward in her mouth and tries unsuccessfully to blow a contemptuous bubble. "I think my conscience would survive any environmental Nuremberg tribunal."

"They deserve —"

"They deserve? That *they* up on the hill? They deserve to be first against the wall when the revolution comes!" She grabs her can of beer from the fencepost and flings it in a high arc toward the house. It lands with several forward bounces before rolling back down the hill and coming to a rest.

She turns to him. After several seconds, he holds his own arm out and drops the plastic onto the ground — as what — a sign of solidarity? She watches him for a moment — he catches her look as she seems to consider him —takes a slow tour of his face, his forward stare, his slow blinks, the fresh streaks in his greying beard, the slight shine of sweat in the bluing depressions under his eyes, the thin break in the tan line along his temple where his sunglasses had been.

"What's up this time? You've been sulking ever since the drive down."

"So, you did notice. So, you are alive." She turns away again, begins to walk along the fence line, trailing a finger along the barbed wire. "I gave you up for dead two hours up the highway. Thought the cruise control was doing all the work. I was scouting the landscape for a suitable spot for your shallow grave — or maybe buzzards. They'd probably be thankful, the buzzards. The pickings look pretty slim around here. Of course, you being a banker, they might spare you out of professional courtesy."

"Ha, ha. That was too easy." He catches up and follows her now random path. "You're off brand. Not up to your usual witty standard."

"You're right," she acknowledges. "Must be the heat."

"Besides, I'm not a banker anymore." He strikes a heroic pose, fists on hips. "I'm a comptroller now."

"Comptroller!" She turns and curtsies to him. "How elegant!"

"Right? I don't count the beans; I count how the beans are counted."

"Sure. But oil, not beans."

"Magic beans."

She looks at him briefly, pushes her gum from cheek to cheek, then turns away again. "I think I liked you better as a banker."

"Really? You said you hated it."

"At the time, sure. You were throwing widows and orphans out into the streets, selling babies for spare parts, but that's just what bankers have done for centuries. One of the amusing quirks of their personalities."

"We have personalities? I never noticed." Feigning shock, he raises a mocking hand to his bosom.

"Touché. Self-awareness. How the mighty have evolved."

"I kind of miss it, too. Banking, I mean. The whole widows and orphans thing was just to please the shareholders," he says, in a conspiratorial whisper. "But," his tone now regretful, "it was a different world from this oil thing."

"No shit."

He thinks back to those insulated days of rules and order. Boring. Predictable. Jacket and tie. Rules and order. Oddly calming. "But I had to get out — we talked about it. There was no room for advancement with all the cutbacks and restructuring. But here — now —" He moves in front of her, adopting the energy and timbre of a professional pitchman. "There's a lot more money in oil. Which means a lot more opportunities for us — a chance to get ahead of the game — do the things we want."

"But now you're in a world run by children," she counters, putting her hand on his chest, as if feeling for a heartbeat. "And childish impulses fuelled by a lack of accountability. Doesn't that bother you?"

"Life is easier when it's predictable?"

She smiles at him, pats his cheek lightly. "It's your role to be predictable."

A sudden bird chorus causes her to turn toward the far trees — catch sight of a minor murmuration — hundreds of birds moving as one in a sweep out of cover, then high into the air, then low and past the far road before disappearing into a fresh stand of poplars. And then, beyond the birds, her look locks on something else.

"Look over there." She points.

"What's on your hand? What have you been painting?"

"Just look. There! Past the County Road. A grain elevator!" And he hears a wistfulness in her voice again. "Another dinosaur. I thought they'd torn all of them down. Grain elevators, I mean, not dinosaurs. There's still plenty of dinosaurs around. But I thought grain elevators were obsolete — that they'd all been sacrificed in the name of progress — economic efficiencies — downsizing/right-sizing/sidestepping/goose-stepping economic trickle down/trickle-up-yours indecent profits. I should Google that. Grain elevators."

"Maybe Clark and Jocelyn had it built especially — for the view," he says, matching her tone of wonderment.

"Or as warning to others. The agrarian underclass."

She takes her phone out of her pocket — looks at it, shakes it, holds it up to the sky. "Dead," she says. "No reception. Even the electrons have drawn a moral line."

"It's the elevation. We're down in a hollow. Come back up to the house. They have wi-fi reception there."

"No." She stuffs her phone back in her pocket. "I can't accept their charity."

"You accepted their beer."

"That . . . is different."

"Is it?"

"It has to be."

"I brought you some more of those sour beers you like."

He turns around to where he'd dropped the bag, picks it up, offers it to her — one handle across his open hand, the other loose, the bag yawning its contents. She looks from it to him.

"Won't they be missed?"

"You're the only one drinking them."

"Great. I've been profiled."

"Everyone else is drinking Coors or Labatt's. Wine coolers —"

"For the ladies."

"For the ladies!" they sing in mocking unison.

"I made sure Clark had a few sours on hand for you."

"Thank you."

"Thank Clark."

"Thank *you*," she replies, with an emphasis that rings odd on his ear. She takes a can from the bag, pulls the tab, holds it away from herself as the first few fizzes roll down the side. She shifts the can to her left hand, shaking the beer from her right. "How did you know I'd be all the way down here?" She licks an errant drop from her fingertips.

"I had a hunch."

"Really? You've ridden this train wreck before?"

He sees the taste of sour on her face, puts the bag at the base of his post.

"I had a hunch. There's something bothering you. You needed to be alone. And you're being funny. You're funnier when there's something bothering you."

"Now I *am* being profiled."

"No. It's just how you process things: tear the world down so you can put it back together in the right order. I can see what you're tearing down, but what are you processing — that I can't figure out."

"Nothing."

"Nothing?" He challenges.

She looks at him again for a long while — long past the point where he begins to get uncomfortable and fidget.

"What?"

"You're aging."

"Jesus —"

"No, no, no. It shows you're vulnerable. Human. It's a good thing. You can see it there," she points, "the bags under your eyes.

The flecks of grey starting to sprout randomly. The loonie sized bald spot growing on the crown of your head."

"I'm the target now? Look, just figure out whatever it is you need to figure out. Obviously, you don't want to tell me. You know where to find me when you need me."

He kicks the bag, watches several cans roll downward to become caught in ruts and tangles of long grass. The bag billows like a lost cloud before snagging on the barbed wire. He backs away toward the house. She watches his first few strides, then turns away to lean again on a fence post, so he turns away as well, continuing up the slope.

"Oh, and you need a haircut." She calls after him. "There'll be fresh hell to pay with the man-children in the oil company if you start looking like a hippie. A man-bun woke environmentalist. A goddamned queer," she announces, in a theatrical accent somewhere between Boston and the Bronx. "No, not queer. They wouldn't say queer. Too evolved. Not offensive enough. Fairy? Yeah, Clark would probably still say fairy. Or maybe something more classic. Nancy-boy!" she adds, triumphantly.

"This isn't the 1950s," he says over his shoulder.

"Isn't it?"

He turns slowly, comes part-way back to stop a few paces behind her.

"You know what you are?"

"Observant? No. You probably had another word in mind. Something short and crisp. A hard consonant like a punch."

"I have never — I would never —" She has hurt him. He sees the look of surprise on her face — at not just the doing, but the why.

"Then why don't you tell me what I am? I need to know." Her eyes begin to well. "Right now, I really need to know. Maybe I'll print it in block letters on a name tag and stick it on my left boob. *Hello: My name is Kate. I'm a . . .*" her voice begins to falter, tears seeping in through the cracks "— but what am I?"

He goes to her, puts his hands gently on her shoulders, tries to look beneath the surface of this broken moment, scratch down to something that makes sense.

"Who are you? You're my wife. And I'm your husband. You're an artist. And you're insane," he adds, and he sees a trickle of a smile, hears a half-sobbed chuckle. "And that's okay. It's another one of your charms. Maybe the one I like best." He pulls her close. She rests her head against his chest. "But let's not do this here."

"Do what?"

"I don't know. Whatever this is." He holds her at arm's length again. "Let's go back up to the house. I mean, it's got to be forty degrees in this sun."

"Yes, it is." She pushes away. "You're sweating. I'm sweating. Leave a dog in a car under conditions like this and the villagers would string you up from the nearest tree — hopefully one of the natural, old-growth ones down here and not the spindly little ornamental fruit trees they've had architecturally inseminated up there." She begins to shout up the slope towards the house. "There's not enough natural water for them — did you know that, Jocelyn? Your trees lack the structural integrity for a good, old-fashioned stringing up!"

"Kate —"

"Go! Go have your steak." She waves him away. "God forbid the cow died in vain."

When he finally speaks, the words are slow, rhythmic, punctuated.

"Is it about the car?"

And he sees the light drain from her eyes over measured, blinkless seconds.

"Now, why would it be about the car?" she begins slowly. "Regardless of how much you overpaid for that sporty little penis extension. That sex-toy with radials. That V-8 vibrator."

"You don't understand. The company paid out these quarterly bonuses. I wasn't expecting it —" but he feels like he is slipping on gravel — the traction of his thoughts spinning impotently.

"So you bought a car."

"Clark said I couldn't keep driving our old rust bucket —"

"The Honda."

"It was almost ten years old."

"So is our relationship. Does Clark think you should be upgrading that too?"

"That's not the same thing."

"So, you come home yesterday with that thing. So flashy. So sleek. So German. God, its backend is smaller than mine."

"Clark said it would be a nice surprise — to show how well we're doing, how good things are going to be."

"Clark is just full of surprises."

"But you're right. It was stupid."

"Stupid. Yes. Like your need to fit in with the young toughs at the company by imitating their immature excesses. How burning more oil is good for the company's bottom line. How what Clark tells you is more important than what I may think. Or maybe you think I don't understand where your priorities are?"

"Priorities. We're talking about my priorities now?"

"I think the car is a pretty clear indication of your priorities."

He tilts his head to one side, waiting for her to continue. She meets his head tilt and offers a brief, sweeping hand gesture.

"A sports car?" Nothing. "A two-seater?" Still nothing. She straightens and sighs, a prosecutor summing up. "So. In your opinion, we'll never need more than two seats. There'll never be more than two of us?"

"Not never."

"Not. Never." The words are stones. "For the full term of the loan then, or however you comptrollers think. Well. You made your decision. Our decision. You voted with our chequebook — your chequebook, you probably feel, given the fiscal imbalance in our incomes. Clark's chequebook, apparently."

"I didn't —"

"Didn't! . . . What? Think? Share? Communicate?"

"Okay," he offers. "Yes. I should have —"

"Do I not matter? Does my opinion not count for anything in this relationship?"

"Look, it was shitty of me. I get it," he fumbles. "But is this about more than the car? What's going on?"

"Nothing."

"Has this got anything to do with the whole *you-turning-thirty* thing?"

"Fuck off. Really?" She looks around, open-mouthed, as if a sniper had just taken her out with a lucky shot from the far tree line. "That's where you want to take this?"

He feels the air cool perceptibly as a cloud bank sweeps across the sun — the sudden grey shadows, the sudden change in detail and texture.

"It's just that you've been —"

"Fuck off. What? I've been what? Never mind. Fuck off."

She throws her beer can at him. He ducks, but the liquid pinwheels from the can and leaves a sweep of red across his shirt.

"Okay. Yes. You're right." He dabs at his shirt, stares at his sticky, red palm.

"No. What have I been? Go on. You're dying to tell me. Or maybe you'll just have Cynthia send me an official email complete with your digital signature."

"Look, I wasn't the one who —"

"I said I was sorry about your fucking sunglasses, okay? But who the hell wears them like that? On the back of their head?"

"It's just —"

"— a place to keep them, I know. It's what all the other man-children are doing. It's how Clark was wearing them — and God forbid you're not a team player." And he sees Clark for a moment, as she must have — Clark — in his *Stuburt Fulmer* golf shirt stretched tight over the beginnings of a paunch, his khaki cargo shorts, his shades planted firmly on his head, backwards, as his neighing laugh caused sonic ripples in the Olympic-sized swimming pool. "Well, it looks stupid," she continues. "He looked stupid. Like he didn't know if he was coming or going. That idiot should have been wearing them dangling below his chin like a drool cup."

"Can we just stay on one topic for a minute? First my job, then the car, then the sunglasses. You say you want to communicate, but when it comes down to actually —" his hands go up, palms outward — the universal sign for *just chill out*, as if that had ever been effective.

"Float me a line of credit and I'll buy you another pair of those unpronounceable Italian sunglasses, if that's what makes you happy — makes you young — allows you to fit in. For that price, you'd think they'd be more aerodynamic."

"Or shock resistant?"

"At least they respond to shock."

"Meaning?"

"When I bumped them to the ground, I didn't know they'd shatter on the paving stones. In front of all your little friends. In front of all the little Clark wannabes."

"Bumped."

"It was an accident."

"It was your elbow."

"It was an accident!" Now her hands go up — the universal sign for *what the fuck*. "I'm not the one who seems to think that everything should be logical, balanced, organized, methodical, systematic — sorry, running out of accounting clichés. I should have saved up when I was young. Opened a linguistic savings account. Then I'd have the words I need now to let you know what an ass you can be." Her hands drop to her sides. "Look, never mind. You're the one who makes the decisions. The privilege of being older. More mature. Steadily employed. A man. I should just sit back, shut up, and enjoy your regression into backwards politics and backwards sunglasses, and the surprise two-seater ride."

She pulls the wad of gum out of her mouth.

"Nicotine gum," she spits. "Like this shit's going to do any good. I shouldn't chew it; I should just roll it up and smoke it."

She rolls the gum into a ball — reaches to stick it to one of the posts.

"Do you have to —"

"What?"

"Never mind."

"Oh. Is this better?"

She puts the gum on the end of her index finger and with a slow, exaggerated gesture presses it onto the tip of her nose like a pink, masticated clown nose.

"Stop it."

"Don't you want me to look pretty?" She twirls twice, her hands skyward, her hips swaying with each revolution. "No?"

She pulls the gum from her nose and sticks it to a fence post. The heat wraps around them as the sun returns, and she fans herself with her open hand, like an extra in *Gone With the Wind* or a lead in one of the lesser-known Tennessee Williams plays.

"I just thought I should look pretty for you." She looks down at herself, smooths her wrinkled shirt. "I tried — I did — but you married an artist with no fashion sense. Maybe I should do my nails in a different colour." She fans her right hand, allowing the sun to flash off her nails. "What colour is this? Pink, maybe. Nicotine on these two. Maybe I should do them in black. Didn't Cynthia have black? Hmmm? Weren't her nails black? And long? And tapered?"

She crouches by her bag, fumbles a pack of cigarettes out, removes one and a small plastic lighter, tossing the pack back in her bag. "Or maybe your eyes were focused somewhere else. But then who could tell what you were looking at behind those expensive shades."

"What are you even —" he reels back for a moment. "Cynthia is just a coworker."

"I'm just trying to figure out what's important to you. I used to know — at least I thought I did, Wait." She reaches into her pocket and takes out a toonie. She drops to one knee and offers the coin up on open palm. "Here. My treat. Buy yourself something pretty. Happy Second Anniversary."

"That's not till next week," he replies, his lips pursed, his diction precise.

"No, you're right. I may need this." She closes her hand, puts the coin back into her pocket. "It's the one I brought into the marriage, so we're even." She turns away again, tries to light her cigarette, shielding the lighter from the nonexistent wind, flicks it repeatedly, ineffectually. "Jeez. Maybe I should go back to the barbeque, if only to light my smoke."

"Look, if you want me to go, I'll go. But right now, you barely let me get a word in edgewise, and everything I do say you weaponize against me."

"No. Stay." She pauses a moment, offers quietly. "I want you here."

"Why? As your punching bag?"

"I guess. Maybe. I don't know." She begins to pace randomly around the grass, flicking the lighter absentmindedly. He follows behind.

"I'm sorry."

"For forgetting our anniversary?"

"I didn't forget. It hasn't happened yet!"

"For the car, then?"

"Yes. That was dumb."

"For Cynthia?"

"No. What does Cynthia have to do with anything?"

"Nothing. You're right. This is not her fault. This is not her fight. She's probably got enough fights of her own."

"Then at least tell me what the hell is going on — you owe me that. Let me in on the workings of your mind —"

And she stops suddenly, still facing away. He sees her take a long, full breath. Her words float high on her slow exhale.

"Maybe go ask Clark."

"Clark? My boss? Ask him what?"

And now she turns, faces him, but not. She seems to want to look at him, at his eyes, but instead her sight drifts upward. And then her words come as an explosion.

"Ask him if he should be cornering the wives of his employees as they come out of the downstairs bathroom. Ask him if he should be pushing them against the wall and pressing himself against them. Ask him if he should maybe keep his tongue in his own mouth?"

Then she lets her sight find its way back to him.

"What the fuck — did he — what the fuck?"

"It was right after I broke your sunglasses. I was embarrassed — ran downstairs. He must have followed me."

"What happened? Are you okay?"

"Nothing happened!" — and as she continues, as he hears her words, he sees her in the hallway — how it must have been — the wall pushing against her back as if complicit — "I froze. For a moment it felt like I wasn't there anymore. That I'd ceased to exist. Then suddenly I was there again and I shoved him away" — her words continue to tumble out, recreating her reaction, the mosaic of the moment — Clark bouncing against the far wall — the framed jersey behind him suddenly askew — her drink can slamming against the drywall by his head — the fine mist of pressure escaping from the bent metal — "then I ran up the stairs. I ran away. Me. I ran away."

She drops to the ground, holds her head in her hands.

"What did he —" and now he feels helpless, his shoulders hunch as he stands small over her.

"He just laughed" — and Jordan knows Clark's laugh — hears it as it must have been — as she took the stairs two at a time — the sound hoarse, triumphant, practiced, slamming into the back of her head like a blow, forcing her to stumble to one knee on the landing. "He yelled: *It was just a joke, bitch* as I ran into the kitchen" — and he hears the vulgar, sexist, entitled, testosterone-driven joke, like all the others he's heard, as she scrambled to her feet — "as I ran away," she whispers to herself.

"That fucker! I'm going to punch his fucking face in!"

"What good will that do?" Her voice is intense, calm — a calmness that unsettles him further — that reframes his rage into naïvité. "He doesn't care. He knows you need this job. You might feel better, but it won't fix anything. It won't change anything."

He sits next to her, moves a hand hesitantly, lightly, to her shoulder.

"Then you can report him."

"Ha! To who? HR? He owns the company. He owns HR."

"The police."

"Right. A party. Drinking. My word against his. The owner of an oil company against a fulltime arts administrator making part-time wages. The word of an artist. I might as well write it out as a Haiku for all anyone would listen." Her voice is crumpled, drunk with a distant laugh. She offers a wry smile to him. "Did you know that the first five syllables of any sentence are the beginning of a Haiku?"

"What? What has that got to do —"

"Nothing. It has nothing to do with it. But here's the start of my Haiku," she says, as she counts each syllable, rhythmically, walking her fingers up the front of his shirt. "I. Did. Tell. Some. One." Her voice, smaller now, startles him.

"Who?"

"Jocelyn. She was at the top of the stairs when I ran up. I said her husband had sexually assaulted me — she looked at me like I'd shit in her bronzer — she flipped her five-hundred-dollar hairstyle, smiled her reconstructed teeth, clenched her Brazilian Butt Lift and said 'You must be mistaken.' Mistaken. Like I'd picked the wrong eyeshadow for my skin undertone — her soooo practiced words, but with that ripple of *not this again* marring the unblemished surface."

"She didn't understand."

"She understood. It's not her first time. But she's learned how to bury it."

Kate tries again to light her cigarette, flicking the spark wheel again and again to no effect — finally hurling the lighter past the fence into the field. She takes the cigarette out of her mouth, breaks it like a promise, throws it to the ground at her feet. And as she looks at it there — as he watches her stare at this perfect white cylinder, now a broken checkmark — the tiny shreds of tobacco spilled on the ground like entrails with no future to portend — it seems to him that she is the saddest thing he has ever seen, the most helpless. And then she begins to cry. She looks up and over to him, as the tears come in sobbing waves. He hesitates only a moment — at this moment he's never seen before — then reaches out, pulls her close.

"Babe, I'm sorry. I'm so sorry," he whispers into her hair. The familiar — the smell of her shampoo, the way her hair curls against his face, the small bone that juts at the base of her neck — they are all so ordinary, so human, that they break his heart. "I wish I could fix this. I'll do something. I'll figure out something. Don't cry. He's not worth it."

"I'm not crying because of that! I've had animals paw me before." Her voice is muffled and distant. "I'm crying because he's bigger than me. By any measure. He has his money, his status. His mansion on the hill. His goddamn pickup truck that could house a village of homeless."

"Don't take it all on yourself. It's nothing you did."

"It feels like it is — like I brought this on myself."

"You didn't. It's not just you."

And for a moment she goes still in his arms.

"What do you mean?"

"He's done this before — with the female staff."

She pushes him away. He tries to hold her again, but she pushes harder, slapping at him. He blocks her swings, but one lands hard, staggering him momentarily.

"What is it? What's wrong?"

"You knew! That he was fucking around? He's a sexual predator and you knew?!"

She gives him one last shove and turns away as he stumbles back, answering her from the ground.

"I heard things. A couple of the guys told me they walked into the coffee room one time and he had Rita against the counter."

"And they did nothing?"

"They didn't have to do anything. He saw them, stepped back. He laughed. Said, *I like a little sugar with my coffee*, and Rita left the room. That was the end of it."

"The end of it."

"Yeah. I mean I never actually saw anything myself."

"So, because you never saw anything, it never happened?"

"No — I mean — the guys would say things sometimes. And sometimes Rita would seem a little nervous if he asked her to stay behind in the boardroom after a meeting."

And as he says it he can see her — Rita — this woman Kate's never met — this woman too afraid to come to the barbeque. And in a sudden wave, he recognizes her helplessness — their helplessness, Rita and Kate — their uncertainty, their feeling of being lost, the fatigue that comes from the long line of unearned fights.

"And you just let it keep happening?"

"Rita never said anything," he says, more a realization than a statement. "Neither did Cynthia. They seemed fine. They didn't say anything, so why should any of us make a big deal of it?"

"Jesus!"

"What could we have —"

He sits with his elbows on his knees. She turns away, walks along the fence line, putting distance between them. He rises from the ground, brushes the grass from his legs as a way to avoid her look.

"Don't! Don't go there! Don't pretend you had no choice. Don't pretend that you were waiting for someone else to do something first. Don't pretend that because you never saw anything you didn't have an obligation to do something."

"Sure. But —"

"You could have done something. You could have asked questions. You could have raised holy shit! You could have quit!"

"I guess I could have."

"You *could* have?" She pivots back to him.

"I — I mean I should have — done something. But it never went too far."

"Too far?"

"From what the guys said. It was just a —"

"What? Just a what? A joke?" She takes a step toward him. "Go ahead, say it." Then another. "I dare you."

"The others just —" he sees the anger in her eyes, the weight of frustration. "— people just laughed it off."

"People?"

"The guys."

"The guys just laughed. And you? You laughed?" She begins to shake, wrapping her arms around herself, her voice fragile as if small pieces were flaking off. "You stood there in the break room with your coffee cup and your doughnut, listened to the story and laughed with the rest of them?"

"No." He looks at her — so small, so diminished — looking at him with something like fear in her eyes. And he knows anything but the truth will crush her further. "Yes."

Her body seems to convulse, then settle into a ragged calm. She looks at him, rising to her full height.

"So, you were part of it all. Just because you weren't in the room when it happened doesn't mean you're not complicit in this whole bullshittery."

"Bullshittery?"

"You fucking heard me."

"I'm sorry. I'm so sorry. As I say it all out loud now — yes. I played a part in it all. I laughed. But I'm not laughing now."

"Why?"

"Because."

"Because?"

"I get it."

"Because you get it?"

"Because now —"

"Now?"

"Now . . . it's affected the person I love most in the world."

For a long moment she is still again, her calmness becoming something solid, cold.

"Yes, it has. The person you love most in the world. The person who finds herself reassessing how she feels about you. The comptroller who couldn't measure what was important."

She moves back to her bag, fumbles for another cigarette. She stares at it before putting it in her mouth, unaware she has no lighter — that it is lost in the grass.

He brushes more dirt from his leg but stops, staring at the ground. His mouth is full of the dryness of the air; grit seems to have settled in his throat. He pulls the words up from somewhere deep and they chill him with their touch.

"I'm sorry that I didn't ask any questions or say anything when I heard the stories. I'm sorry I did nothing."

"So maybe you should start thinking about what you should do."

"I'm sorry he hurt you."

"He didn't hurt me. He made me a cliché. That's worse. He made me just another in a long line of faceless, powerless nobodies. That's not who I am. I am not a faceless nobody. I am not powerless!"

She glances briefly at him, then away across the fields. He sees her eyes click onto some spot in the distance. Everything in the world seems to stop. Then, in a single motion, she flicks her cigarette away and moves to the fence.

"What are you doing?"

"Look over there."

"Where?"

"There. There!"

He joins her at the fence — looks out to what appears to be a ragged tree line, but is in fact a series of clusters — brush and copses oddly spaced side to side and front to back so there are several hidden gaps. And through these gaps now wander dozens of cows, fanning out into the field in the foreground, as if on cue, as if they had held their entrance until this precise moment, as if they knew, collectively, that they were needed.

"The cattle. They just moved into the field from someone's pasture, probably behind those trees."

"The cows?"

"The Holsteins." She takes the rag from her back pocket and picks up the two small cans of paint — one black, one white — from the ground. She holds his look intently, then pushes the bag into his hands. "Look at them. They're perfect."

"Christ. You're not going to —?"

"I don't expect you to understand."

"The cows?"

"Holsteins!"

"Now? But we were just talking about — you were just —!" But he has seen this before, this seemingly irrelevant pushback — this art as a shield — and he stumbles in his thoughts. "What if they come down here —"

"They're not going to come all the way down here. They'd have to catch the *3:10 to Yuma*."

"What — the what —"

She's at the three-strand barbed wire, placing the cans on the far side.

"A movie. 1957. Glenn Ford. 2007 remake with Russell Crowe? A little help here."

He moves to her — holds the top strand up, the second down, creating a gap for her to squeeze through. "I'm going to paint them."

"Do you have to?"

"It's what I do."

"But they're cows."

"It's my art. You married an artist. Has two years of marriage taught you nothing? Two years. Ha! Probably feels more like twenty-four months to you."

"But they're cows." he replies, flicking her shirt free from the barb that held her then steps back, his look downward, his stance shifting.

"You're embarrassed."

"They're cows. You're going to smear paint on them. Can't you paint them the regular way — on a canvas? What if someone sees? What if they see?"

"They have a genetic blind spot to art. But look at those. Perfect."

He looks at the fifty or so black and white animals. Some are still; some shift slowly as if trying to find their mark; some look her way expectantly, as if the show must go on.

"Look," she marvels. "Look how each one is different. The pattern of light and dark on each is unique. Now look — there — on the left. Those two have moved a little, changing their position relative to each other and relative to the rest. Whatever pattern existed prior — just a moment ago — is gone. The sequence of black and white against the landscape has changed and will never be repeated again. You can see that, can't you?"

"Yes — maybe. On one level it's numbers: permutations and combinations."

"Yes! Chance — plain and simple. Add to that the patterns, the geometric. That the mathematical is also driving the visual — that's art. Performance art, really."

"Okay. But who's going to —"

"— to see it? No one, maybe. Or if someone does, do they even give a shit."

"Exactly!"

"If I worried about how many people might see it, or what they might think, I wouldn't be much of an artist."

Again, their eyes meet and hold. He knows he should say something — he is supposed to say something — and his mouth opens in preparation — but he makes the mistake of taking too long to choose his words. She turns, cans of paint in hand — moves rapidly across the open field.

He watches her — her purposeful stride. He thinks back to her other schemes, other projects, none of which ever made any sense to him, none of which would ever make her a dime or earn a line of recognition. But he also feels something familiar, something deeper inside: the grudging respect, the morbid interest, that her ideas always evoke in him.

"But why paint them?" he calls. "Why not leave them as they are, if they're already art?"

She stops, still facing away. He can see her shoulders tense before she turns.

"That's the point." She takes two steps back to him. "They have a pattern now — each of them. I add to it, revise it — just one or two — just an extra spot here, extend a shadow there. Just enough that it's different than it was, but not so much that anyone would notice — not the farmer, not anyone driving by. If I do it right, they won't even know I've been here."

"We can get you other cows."

"No. It has to be these cows."

"We must have passed a hundred pastures on the way down."

"It has to be these cows! It has to be now! I need this, Jordan."

"Okay. But —" he struggles "— if it's already art — natural art — and you change it —"

"It's the changing of it that elevates the art."

"And if no one is supposed to see —"

"The point is that it's not permanent, in any aspect. It's perfect impermanence. The pattern of the cows in the field, in relation to each other. My paint fading or being washed away by rain or sweat, or one cow rubbing against another, transferring portions of the art to the other. It takes the infinite possibilities of nature and adds another layer of infinite possibilities — and meanwhile it's all returning to the original. The entropy — the internal transformation of the system as a whole — is the art."

She turns and continues away.

"But —"

"Whatever."

"— you're painting cows!"

"Whatever!" A backward hand waves in his direction.

"Is this how you're going to deal with —"

"He doesn't know who I am." She calls back to him, her stride unslowed. "He tried to make me small. He tried to erase who I am. This is who the fuck I am!"

He watches as she continues across the field. He watches as she approaches the first cow, slowly, one open hand extended as in alien greeting. He expects it to run, or at least shy from her touch, but the cow, in turn, observes her contentedly, chewing it over. She dips her other hand in a can of paint, reaching forward to extend a dark patch into the surrounding light with rubs and caresses.

"Just another Saturday night painting cows in the field."

ACT TWO

Jordan sits on the field side of the fence, his back against one of the wooden posts, several empty beer cans beside him. The afternoon sun has swung a wide arc, and he had been asleep for most of it — but now he nods awake, feeling where the bright red sunburn blazes across one side of his face. Her bag still rests in his lap like a contented dog.

Through sleepy eyes, he watches Kate approach slowly — floating it seems — toward the fence from across the wide field. She is splattered with paint and dirt. And she is happy.

She pauses at the fence line to turn and look back at the cows again — likely to admire her now unseen efforts — then slips between the fence's barbs and stops behind him, looking down.

"You look so peaceful," she says. "Contended. Childlike." Her voice, above him, seems distant, dreamlike. "The shadow of youth has floated up through your years as you slept."

"Is that a quote from some distant English lit class?" he yawns, rises, turns, leans on a post.

But instead of answering, she gently eases her bag from his restful grip and puts the can of black paint away. But the white she opens. She dips the tips of her fingers in and paints, with the lightest of touches, a white line down his left cheek. He raises a hand to his face — the thick stickiness on his skin.

"Really? You're painting *my* face now?"

"How now, brown cow? It's just following the smile lines." He rubs at his face, smearing more than cleaning. "Come here," she offers, taking the rag from her back pocket and rubbing his face, gently, like a mother with an errant child.

"Do you want to touch up my bald spot?"

She laughs. "It'll probably take at least two coats." They lean forward, foreheads touching, the fence between them.

"You're finished with the cows?"

"See for yourself."

She turns to put the rag away and leans the bag against one of the posts. She rotates the can of white paint slowly, nervously, in her hand as he scans the sixty-degree array of cattle.

"I don't see any difference."

"Then my work here is done. I'll take that as a compliment."

"Look, if I can't — if I know what you've done but there's no way even I can —" but he pauses, shifts his weight from one foot to the other, rubs at the paint on his hand.

"Go on."

"It's about seeing. And being seen. This is another of your alternative art things."

"Yes."

"Like before, with the canvases — the blank canvases."

"Yes," she says. "The only alternative to art was the lack of art."

"Which is why you started leaving the canvas blank."

"Yes."

"Entirely blank."

"Yes."

"Except for your signature."

"Yes," she replies, shifting uncomfortably. "In my defense, it was written in white on a white background."

"And when we met — ten years ago — you were in that band. The whole band just standing there on the stage, full instruments, speakers, mics, everything —"

"Playing nothing, yes."

"For three twenty-minute sets. The only true alternative to music being —"

"— no music. That's why our CD —"

"— was blank. I still don't get that."

"You bought three copies."

"Gifts."

A silver SUV appears from down the far Range Road, a bridal train of gravel billowing behind. She leans on the wire of the fence, watches it for the ninety seconds it takes to approach, pass by and disappear into the next low. He spends the time looking at her — at the eagerness in her face, how her eyes brightened then dimmed, like an imitation of the vehicle's Doppler sound.

"I don't think they even looked." She is quiet, wiping at the tears the dust has drawn from her eyes.

"It doesn't matter."

"There was only one person in the car, and they didn't even look."

"You said it doesn't matter."

"Right. It doesn't matter," she repeats.

"It doesn't matter. At that speed —there's no way they could even —" an idea strikes him, and he fumbles to take his phone out of his pocket — activate the camera — catch the bovine scene in a video clip.

"Don't!"

"I just want to capture it."

She slips through the wire, puts a hand on his arm. "That's not the point. That's exactly the opposite of the point. It doesn't matter."

"But — it feels like it does matter to you."

"It — doesn't — shouldn't — matter!"

"It feels like maybe just this once you wanted to be seen."

She drops to the ground, sitting back against one of the posts. He sits against the next post over. The light has faded — the sun low and dipping behind the tree line. They sit in silence for several seconds, feel some edge of coolness sneak back into the air. She turns to him, then turns away — and he remembers the drive down — so long ago now, when all Kate was angry about were small things — how she had held up her index finger, touching the inside of the windshield while he drove — tracing a random rain path as they passed through the briefest of squalls and then back into sun.

And he sees how she's slumped now, suddenly weary of it all — weary of all the rage. He recognizes her far-away stare.

Silence seeps into the cracks, pushing time aside like sand. He reaches over, takes the can of white paint from her hand, dips his fingers in and gently adds a line to her face.

"How now, brown cow?" he says, and she laughs, slides over beside him. "What does that even mean?"

"You're right. Brown cows are boring. Limited opportunity for contrast. Uninteresting." She kisses him gently on the cheek. "We are not brown cows. You are not a brown cow."

"Thank you." He looks over at the cows, receiving several languid stares in return while others graze with a deliberate intensity. "If the point of the art is not to be noticed, then I would have thought that the lack of contrast on a brown cow would add to the obscurity and make it more interesting — as a work of art."

She pauses longer than he knows she would have liked.

"A cute bit of logic. But there's no risk. The point isn't that your work isn't seen — that your touch, the mark you leave, isn't seen — it's that it could be seen if only the world would stop what it's doing and observe what's right in front of it. It's like Holmes' eternal chiding of Watson: *you see, but you do not observe.*"

He shifts against the post, shrugging into a smoother curve of the wood.

"All art exists in a transient moment," she continues, "some more than others. Theatre is of the moment — there, then gone. The closer to transience, the closer to art."

"I still don't get it."

"No shit, Sherlock," she laughs.

As darkness begins, the low light draining into the rough grass of the fields, the cows begin to shift, haphazardly it seems, back to the hidden pasture from which they came — as if the darkness were the curtain descending — the show over.

She reaches back for her bag, fumbles for her cigarettes. She takes one, puts it in her mouth. He shifts closer to her.

"I watched you, you know, as you painted your cows. How you rested one hand on the cow to calm it — as if to ask if it was okay — while you dipped your other hand in the can of paint. The way the cow turned away, seemed about to take a step or two, then reached down to pull another clump of grass and weed into its mouth with a kind of *oh, this again* look. As if, to them, it was the most natural thing in the world — like your art was communicating with them — like it was a conversation."

"Maybe you do get it."

She reaches over and takes his hand.

"Did you talk to them, the cows?"

"Yes. I explained to them that nothing I did to them would be lasting. That our interaction wasn't permanent. That some people will see them, but more will not. And they told me to remember how beautiful the world is — how beautiful it can be. How just north of here the landscape transforms. Rain-greened fields rolling on to the crest of the horizon. Time stirring and billowing in the evening mist that hangs over the low pools, blending upward into the over-hanging trees, like fingers through hair."

"That's beautiful."

"Some I told my troubles. They're good listeners."

"Did you talk about me?"

"Yes. But only because they asked. I told them I thought I was losing you — that you were being seduced over to the dark side." She looks up at the sky for a moment, long blinks. "They told me that I should trust that you were better than that." She looks to him. "I feel better now," she says. "I feel . . . in control again. This is something he could never take away."

He picks up his phone.

"There's no service," she reminds him, but he continues, unlocks the screen, holds the phone up to the sky. "Worried?"

"What? No."

"I mean about your job?"

"No. It's just —I wrote a text to the group. Told them I quit. Told them why. Got a post ready for the company Facebook page. Maybe when they read what I wrote — once we get up the hill a bit and I can send it — maybe others will quit as well."

"My hero." Her voice goes flat, her look dulls. He drops his hand. She begins to pick at the paint flecks between her thumb and forefinger.

"Want to see it?"

"No."

"I thought you'd be happy."

She pauses, looks to where the cows had been, speaks slowly. "I am happy. But now I find out that while I was happily painting my cows, you were doing important things. Saving the world. My big, strong man. My world shouldn't need saving. I shouldn't need to worry, every day, about whether how I dress or how I've done my hair, or whether I smile will bring me unwanted attention. I shouldn't need a heroic act to survive a company barbecue. Art should be the heroic act."

"But I'm not quitting just because of you. I spelled it out: you, Rita, Cynthia, the open secrets everyone laughs about — the whole thing. I called him out as a predator. That I'm ashamed of the way I just stood by — that we should all be ashamed for just standing by."

"So, you would quit over this. You would become the impulsive one."

"I could use a change."

"Couldn't we all? "

"Isn't that enough?"

"It's a start." She rubs at the paint smear on her palm. "As long as we're reversing roles, let me be the practical one. What will we do for money?"

"I'll get another job."

"It could take a while. And we won't last long on what I make. Relying on an artist for fiscally stability. You might as well be talking to cows."

"Maybe we could sell one of those cows. If you signed it. An original bovine baroque!"

She laughs an honest laugh.

"We'll get by," he continues. "We can sell the car."

"The car?"

"Yeah. Maybe get something more practical. A sedan. A mini-van," he adds, mockingly seductively.

"Let's not get too crazy here," she laughs.

"Fine. But we can sell the car."

"We."

He stands, ducks through the fence and starts to move up the grassed slope, holding his phone in the air again.

"As soon as I get a signal, I'm hitting send."

"Look at you, standing defiant like a warrior, your sword aloft." But then her quiet word stops him cold in his tracks. "Wait."

"What?"

"Maybe you shouldn't quit. Maybe you should stay."

"Stay? Why would I stay?"

"You're good. You're one of the good ones. The cows said so."

He shakes his head. This is not enough for him. He needs logic. He needs facts tightly packed as a foundation to build upon.

"If you leave — even if you inspire a handful of others to leave — things won't get better; they'll probably get worse. He'll just fill the void you've created with more of his own kind."

"It won't stop the assholery."

"The what?"

"You heard me."

"I did," she laughs. She rises and joins him on the freshly mown side of the fence.

"So I should stay — be the subversive in his midst."

"You can be an influence, on the younger staff — use that greying hair for good."

"By just talking. By calling him out. By empowering people."

"You can break him from within. Who knows — maybe you'll even influence Jocelyn."

"But if I challenge him, he'll just fire me," he counters.

"Maybe he won't. Firing you might send the message that you're right, that you're a threat." She shrugs. "And if he does fire you, so what? You've already said you were ready to quit, so he has no power over you. You'd be no worse off than if you'd quit."

"Plus, with a severance cheque. And maybe a settlement!"

She ruffles his hair, like she would a favoured dog.

"Ah, who's my sweet, little fiscally motived do-gooder." He moves to the fence as she continues. "Maybe you'd be a martyr to something bigger."

He leans on one of the posts, absently smoothing his hair back in place, then rolling his phone over in his hand, watching it catch the low angled reflection of the dimming light.

"If I'm going to make any difference, I need a plan. What to say and how to say it."

She turns, standing a few paces behind him.

"It's complicated. It's messy."

"I can do messy."

"And there's no guarantee anything you do will make any difference."

"But it's the trying, right?"

"It all starts with the trying. With the first smear of paint. Start with the storytellers."

"*Hey, guys,*" he says, mimicking his own innocent tone. "*That's not right, what he did. We shouldn't be laughing about it. That's not fair to Rita or Cynthia.*"

"Yes. And if you see Clark doing something —"

"— let him know that someone is watching. To break things up. *What's going on in here*, or, *Hey, Rita, Kyle down in accounting needs you right away.*"

"Yes. And then get more direct."

"*Hey Clark, do you think HR would think this was okay?*"

"Right!" she cheers him on. "Use his name and draw other people into it. *Hey Clark, do you think Jocelyn would think this was okay?*"

"*Hey, guys, am I the only one who thinks what Clark's doing isn't right?*"

And they begin to riff — rattling off examples, goading each other on. Laughing. Laughing until their energy is shaking them where they stand.

"*Does anyone think it's okay that Clark is forcing himself on her?*"

"*That Clark has her pinned against the wall?*"

"*Hey Clark, did she ask you to put your tongue in her mouth?*"

"*Hey Clark, did she ask you to put your hand up her blouse?*"

"*Hey Clark, did she ask you to put your penis in her coffee?*"

"*Hey Clark, is that your penis or were they serving shrimp cocktail in the cafeteria?*"

They laugh together — the kind of laugh that leaves their stomachs sore — the kind of laugh that rings in the quickening dim, answered finally by a distant lowing from the unseen cows that makes them laugh all the more.

"You see? The cows get it." And she returns a brief moo of acknowledgement.

He looks from her to his phone, then presses the screen and sweeps it shut. "Delete."

"And you live to fight another day."

He stuffs his phone away in his pocket, looks back at her, hesitant. "Do you love me again?"

"Oh, my big, blank canvas. I never stopped."

He takes her hand, squeezes it, kisses it, pulls her to him. She reaches forward and wipes paint from his lip.

"I wonder if Clark will still do the fireworks." He scans the sky.

"He would never lose the chance to blow shit up."

He bends down to pick a blade of grass, studying it as he rolls it in his fingers. "I'm sorry about the car. About not talking with you — not including you. That was shitty."

"You driving up to the house in that surprise car made me feel small — not like what Clark did, but still small."

"I see that now." He flicks the blade of grass away, turns to her. "I'm sorry about everything."

"Listen to you — always apologizing — asking me to forgive you. For everything. That's not forgiveness; that's absolution. Do I do that to you? It must be hell."

"Maybe a little."

"I'm sorry."

"For what? You have nothing to be —"

She puts a single finger to his lips and presses gently to stop him.

"I'm sorry," she repeats. "And thank you." Again, they press their foreheads together and there is nothing in the world but the two of them. After a moment she offers to this silence, "Oh, speaking of forgiveness, I need more white paint."

"Too many cows?"

"Sure. And one big ass truck. Clark may be embarrassed to drive around with those rude words painted on it."

He steps back. "You painted Clark's truck?"

"Like a nametag. *Hello, my name is Clark. I am a sex offender with a tiny dick.*"

"The truth is a heavy burden to bear. He'll know you did it."

"It was kids. Joyriding kids."

"*It was kids, officer. Honestly! Joyriding kids.*"

"*They drove off that way — past where those cows are.*"

"*We could hear the kids mooing. They must have been high on something.*"

"*I think they took a left at the grain elevator.*"

She sits on the ground, her back against a post. He follows her lead, his back against the same post, their legs stretched out together up the gentle slope.

"Would you really have punched Clark?" she asks.

"For you? Sure. Once, anyway."

"Only once?"

"I was a banker. Never a day of real work. You know how delicate our hands are." He holds his hands up to the sky, fingers splayed, then daintily flicks a paint speck from his left thumb.

She overlaps her right foot with his left. "I've been thinking about my next project."

"Already?"

"I'm on a roll. You may approve, since it's more removed this time — more arm's length. Less chance for embarrassing encounters with people or farm animals."

"You had me at farm animals. Go on."

"It's going to be cards this time. Christmas cards. On the front will be a typical Christmas scene — a manger with a star above." She paints the idea on the sky with a sweep of her hands.

"That sounds normal."

"Yes! That's it exactly! Normal. It *seems* normal!"

"But —"

"I'm going to send them out — hundreds of them — in the summer," she says, the excitement building in her voice. "To people I don't know. Names chosen randomly from the phone book."

"Do they still have those? Phone books? Like grain elevators."

"Yes! Right? That will add a whole layer of the obscure. I'll have to go to the library and use an old copy of one. Use a name that might no longer be at that address. Someone who might even be dead!" Her enthusiasm is explosive, infectious.

"Freaky!"

"And then the cards — the cards, with no greeting, will be signed simply *Love, Ed and Betty.*"

"And who are —?"

"No one! Get it!?" And she leaps to her feet, kicking off her flip-flops, dancing around the grass, twirling in excitement. "It's performance art, but with the artist removed. Performance art performed by the audience — the recipients — and each response different, as they search their memories for who the hell Ed and

Betty are. Distant cousins, maybe, or that couple they played mahjong with on the cruise ship two winters ago." She pulls him to his feet. "Hundreds of distinct and individual acts of art that the artist will never even see."

"Cool. I think I get it."

She jumps up and he catches her, her legs wrapped around him, leaning back as he twirls her around once, then twice — and she looks at the sky — at the stars now appearing — and he wishes he could remember the names of the constellations so he could name them for her – present them to her as a gift as each comes out of hiding. He stops and she drops her feet to the ground. And they hold each other, and it all makes sense again.

"It's getting dark."

"And quiet," he says, looking up. "Listen."

"I don't hear anything. The music's stopped."

"Exactly."

He steps back, hands in the air, gives one full shake of his body, and begins a stiff, unrhythmic dance.

"What are you —"

"Doing? I'm dancing. Like before. Remember? When we first met." He does an awkward spin, bumping against a post and almost falling. He twirls again, marginally more successfully, and reaches out a hand to her. "Join me."

"I don't —"

"We used to. Every show. Part way through the last set, you'd jump down off the stage, and we'd groove to the silence. Come on!"

He again offers his hand. She takes it and they turn and dip, out of sequence, out of step, but always connected in their awkward movements, in their abandon, in their not-giving-a-shittitude.

"Listen to that non-existent beat!" He gyrates on one foot, kicking the other out with unparalleled ungracefulness.

She bursts out laughing again as she mimics his moves, adding head gestures and jazz hands. "You, my love, are a terrible dancer."

"I take my inspiration from the best. The only alternative to dance —"

"Is to non-dance."

"Dance like no one's watching!" he calls to the sky.

"Dance like no one will ever see!" she yells.

"Dance like you're the 3:10 from Yuma!" he chugs, and they continue to dance, but now both offering up their existential interpretation of a western locomotive under full steam, without a care or talent, but laughing with the pure joy of their abandon.

"We should probably dance our way back to our car," he says, with mild exhaustion and a sad finality. "Make our get away before Clark unleashes the hounds."

"You're funny — again. Probably means you're too drunk to drive."

With a sweeping movement, she reaches into her bag and snatches out the car keys, dangling them in front of him as she sashays out of his reach.

"How did you —"

"You dropped them when you went to pick up your sunglasses. I'll get us home. One of us has to be the responsible adult if this relationship is going to last." She twirls the key ring on her finger like a six-shooter. "Besides, if we're going to sell the car, we should probably drive the shit out of it while it's still ours."

A sudden violent explosion of colour — and then a second and a third — shatters the silence as someone up the hill sets off the first of the fireworks. They freeze in their dance. Then the driving beat of Arsenic Machine thumps from the speakers far away, causing the air to vibrate.

Their heads turn upward in unison to a sky now flashing through colours. They look at each other, fall to their backs on the grass, their heads together as the world bursts apart above them in vivid rainbows of light, laid out solely for their joint amusement.

COFFEE BREAK

The deep grey of the evening was slowly diffusing to a pale grey morning: that shade of grey which made it hard to distinguish where the concrete stopped and the sky began. The autumn cold and colour heralded the death of another year, like the distant sound of traffic horns from what little traffic could be found at that godawful time of day. The sight and feel was as common to him as his soap-filmed face half blind in the morning mirror.

Every day for the last twenty-three years Edgar Walls rolled out of bed at 4:05 in order to shower, shave, and dress, and walk the nine blocks to have his small downtown coffee shop open by 5:30 sharp. This in rain and shine, sun and snow, and in spite of the glaring fact that he had never once, in twenty-three years, had a customer before 7:30.

Oh, the people were out there all right, trudging past his door in intermittent dribbles as they guided their uncooperative bodies to work. Some even paused to look in the window, no doubt taking cold comfort in the fact that some poor bastard was worse off than they, already hard at work.

But no one stopped.

In the old days they had begun their honest working days with hearty homecooked meals: eggs in multiple, bacon, hashbrowns fried golden in the drippings — this was before the invention of cholesterol, before guilt became a side order. Now their loyalties lay beneath the golden arches with the breakfast croissants and layered sausage takeaways of the bright plastic fast-food chains or with the high-end bistros offering Guatemalan blends in Italian sizes. Edgar had also failed to capitalize on this later trend of caffeine as a designer drug, continuing to offer only the industrial strength version in ceramic cups with saucers. In the fickle and turbulent shifts of epicurean life, Edgar had remained constant and immovable, and, as a result, he had been left behind. His clientele had devolved to the gastronomically nostalgic. The kind whose idea of a coffee shop is defined by the black-and-white diners of the late-night movies, where the eggs were greasy and the coffee old enough to move out and get a place of its own. The kind that didn't feel morning started until after nine.

But Edgar wasn't bitter. No. Nor was he blind to the whims of the general public. Neither was tradition his purpose for maintaining his early morning timetable. He enjoyed the morning, that was all. He relished his twin hours of quiet, sipping the first cup from the day's vat, munching contentedly on toast and eggs and bacon, idly flipping through the tabloid version of world events, free from all cares, responsibilities, and his wife.

But today. He could sense something different about today. A strange feeling in the air — an uneasy foreboding in the signs offered by the inanimate objects that shared his solitude. Today the coffee urn neglected to spit out the first ounce of coffee in the random direction of its choosing; today his morning toast popped up even and brown and remained in the machine (rather than leap flaming into the air like some whole wheat shooting star, as was its wont); today the bacon on the grill smelt like — well — like bacon, foregoing its usual distasteful aroma of warming carnage of indeterminable origin and age.

And today, even before the first yolk had surrendered to his probing triangle of toast — even before the minute hand had finished its leisurely stroll to the top of the seventh hour — the bell above the shop door tinkled and a man entered in.

"Good morrow, gentle innkeeper!"

Edgar stared open-mouthed at this sunny greeting, yolk dripping like congealed sunshine from the toast wedge halfway to his mouth.

"Food, food, and tankards of ale for me and my men, for we have ridden far!" he laughed, or quoted — the provenance was unclear — but the gentleman was alone. Edgar was reasonably sure of that, but as the shop bell signalled the closing of the door he counted again. One.

"Come now, my good fellow," boomed the hearty voice. "Look lively, and fetch me sustenance!"

Edgar blinked again, then slowly lowered his toast, with his apprehensions, back to his plate, pushing them both aside. He rose, wiping his hands on his greying apron, then moved behind the counter to the grill.

"Uh, what did you want?"

"Want? Well —"

"Eggs? Bacon? Ham? Sausage?"

"Eggs? Yes, I'll have eggs. Bring me eggs, with their sunny little eyes peering hopefully skyward."

"How many?"

"Hmmm?"

"How many sunny little eyes?"

"Two. Three. No! Four! Make it four. Send word to the chickens near and far: four eggs, and now! And ham."

"Right. I'll tell the pigs. Toast or hash browns?"

"Hash browns, I think. Yes. Potatoes. Apples of the earth — *les pommes de terre*. Precisely. Potatoes."

"Grab a seat. It won't be long."

Edgar moved to the cooler for the eggs and ham, pausing long enough to watch the man's reflection in the glass door. He was tall — quite tall — six-foot-six or -seven, as near as Edgar could judge, but he appeared to weigh less than a hundred and fifty pounds. The clothes he wore were old and ill-fitting, likely not his own: a khaki great-coat, fraying tweed jacket with a badly knotted school tie, dusty cotton trousers, the cuffs split several inches above military-style boots that had long ago forgotten the meaning of a good spit shine (the spit was still there, but not the shine).

The man sat at the booth near the window, carefully pulled the wool gloves from his hands and placed them opposite, so it looked as if another were sitting there but had just stepped away for a moment.

His age? Hard to say. The patchy, greying beard, gaunt face and unkempt appearance suggested the declining side of his thirties, but his lively green eyes and pure exuberance belonged to someone a good deal younger (perhaps borrowed with the clothes?).

"Just passing through?" Edger ventured. The question immediately struck him as inane. He asked it because the man was a stranger. There were almost a million people in the city he had never seen before. Clearly they were not 'just passing through,' except in perhaps a purely metaphysical sense not likely uppermost in most people's mind. The stranger didn't see it that way, though.

"Very astute of you, my man. Yes, I am indeed just *passing through*," he replied, indicating with a pantomime cup that he had no coffee.

"Where you from?"

"Oh, here and there. The world is my home, and I've stayed in many of its rooms."

Alarm bells went off in Edgar's head with piercing intensity. The man was a drifter. Worse than that, he was a drifter with a philosophical leaning — the kind that speaks of freedom and the power of nature and the secrets of the soul, and drinks cleaning products and sleeps in a cardboard box in one of the less-than-fashionable alleys. Edgar could feel the touch for a free meal as tangibly as a tap on the shoulder or a hand on his wallet. He idly filled a mug with coffee and moved casually to the man's booth.

"Hope you weren't thinking of paying for breakfast with a credit card. We don't take credit cards here. Management policy."

"A very wise decision in this day and age. Oh no, I wasn't planning to use a credit card."

"Good. Good. 'Cause we . . . uh . . . don't take them."

Pause. Edgar marshalled his forces for another attack.

"We can't do debit cards either. Machine's down. Been down all morning. Tried phoning the guy, but, well —"

"Technology. Is it really the boon it claims to be? I think not."

"True. True. I don't even have a cell phone."

"How interesting."

"How —?"

"I trust we may come to some manner of arrangement based upon this."

Here the man reached into the depths of his surplus greatcoat and removed a small revolver, placing it with delicacy on the table.

"I realize it's not exactly coin of the realm," he continued, "but its use is common enough these days."

Another pause, and silence so profound Edgar could hear the sound of whitecaps breaking in the cup of coffee clenched in his trembling hand.

Edgar reached out to touch the object — what looked like a surplus service revolver, more at home in a black and white movie. The stranger covered the handle with a light palm. Edgar continued reaching out, touching the blue steel barrel with a single finger.

"Four eggs, right?"

"Correct. And ham."

He placed the cup of coffee down, took two steps backward, then turned to carry out his order. Eggs cracked under the pressure of his grasp, and ham slabs hit the grill with a sizzle. Hash browns, too, hurried to brown, like tiny ball bearings of starch and grease, and a bullet wound of sliced tomato oozed life.

Over the din of activity the man spoke.

"I trust I'm not being an imposition."

"What?"

"An imposition — putting you to any trouble."

"Oh no. No trouble. Happy to oblige. It's why I'm here. It's what I do."

"No. I mean, it's so quiet here, and you were so alone. I know. I've been watching from across the street for a quarter hour or more. I love the quiet. I revel in being alone. Contact with other humans can be so tiresome, don't you think? I greatly fear I have stolen your morning time to yourself."

"Hell no. You caught me on a bad day. By this time the place is usually alive with small arms fire."

"Ah. The gun." He said, as if the conclusion had just become evident, *Quode erat demonstrandum.*

"Yes, the gun. I couldn't help but notice."

"I am most humbly sorry about that — believe me, I am — but the needs of the time . . ." he trailed off.

"You're broke."

"Actually —"

"Look, put the gun away. No need for anyone to get hurt. Breakfast's on me."

"Oh no, really. I couldn't. You don't —"

"I insist. Don't worry about it. I'll find a way to hide it on my taxes."

"No, you don't understand. I won't have earned it."

"No problem. So you dry a few dishes, wipe down a couple of tables — nothing much — and we call it square. So just put the gun away —"

"I'm afraid I can't."

"Why not?"

"Honour will not have been served. The job will not be done."

"Why —?"

"Because I've been hired to kill you."

One of the eggs spat out its yolk in a yellow interpretation of the St. Valentine's Day massacre, and the hashbrowns quietly took on the appearance of entrails drying in the sun.

Sometimes, in conversation, the dialogue is an easy chain of comment/response — more chemical reaction than an exchange of ideas, as specific words act as catalysts to bubble forth the required response. Sometimes the catalyst is added but nothing happens. The chance is missed. The experiment is a flop. This was just such a time. When the catalyst is 'I'm going to kill you,' or any of the countless variations on this universal theme, there are equally countless potential responses, from the aggressive to the religious to the entreating. But Edgar could think of none. Edgar could think of nothing.

He silently brought the man his breakfast, then freshened his cup of coffee and sat on one of the red counter stools, swivelling around to better keep track of the man's actions.

But what actions? He ate in relative silence, save for an occasional smack of enjoyment and an almost continuous humming (some sort of marching tune, Edgar thought). The man's eating habits were comparable to others of their species. There was nothing to betray the man's announced intentions, although Edgar was certain he could discern the hint of a smile on his face as he knifed the ham into tiny pieces.

Finally, the man finished, pushing the plate aside as he popped the last piece of yolk-stained bread crust into his mouth.

"A repast fit for royalty."

"You liked it, did you?" Edgar replied, cleaning away the dirty dishes. "I'm so glad. Somehow, I always thought that last meals were meant to be eaten, not served."

"Oh, very good. Droll, with a tinge of fate unresolved." The man chortled. "Levity in the face of the inevitable. You've risen inestimably in my books. I shall most certainly advise my client that you died like a gentleman."

"Your client?" the reaction began.

"That's correct."

"Who is your client? Who wants me dead?" The question tasted strange in Edgar's mouth.

"Oh. Privileged information, my dear man. Doctors, lawyers, psychiatrists: all we professionals believe that what passes between a client and his counsel is sacred."

"Even before a grand jury?"

"I greatly fear your sense of humour has severe limitations. But, as the ability to smile in the face of death is not exactly a trait one gets the opportunity to practice at length, I will accept the apology I'm sure you were about to offer."

"You're welcome. Don't I have a right to know?"

"Frankly, no."

"Oh."

Silence now, thick enough to fry an egg in.

"So?" Edgar offered.

"So what?"

"So how do we go from here?"

"Ah, the next link in the chain of predestination. Yes. Fine. How indeed? There are procedures in this regard. The rules are quite clear. I think it would be best if you sat over here."

He indicated one of the booths away from the window, the first in the row. Edgar moved to it in a steady and dreamlike way, as one walking the last mile or completing his tax return. He sat facing the door. The stranger moved behind him. Edgar heard the click of the revolver as the hammer was pulled back. The sound was like a clock being set or a winch being lowered or, well, like a gun being cocked — because, he realized, there really was no sound quite like it, especially when experienced in this particular way.

"Tilt your head forward, please."

He did so, closing his eyes as an afterthought. And he saw his life flash before his eyes, the endless parade of mornings, all the same, as if the film of his life had slipped its sprockets on the same stuttering scene. And he thought of his wife — of the small amount in their savings account that would leave her comfortable for a bit, and wondered idly if she'd marry his brother, of whom she seemed inordinately fond. And he found . . . he was okay with this. He held no regrets. He was at peace.

"And now, goodbye, Mr. Wells."

"Walls," he droned.

"I beg your pardon?"

"Walls. Edgar Walls."

His eyes still closed, Edgar heard the rustle of paper and a profanity proffered on the wings of a sigh.

"Is this 9943 — 107 Street?"

"107 Avenue, yes," he replied, eyes still closed to it all.

Again a mumbled curse, this time followed by the rushed scrape of worn-out boots on warped linoleum, the sound of coins bouncing on a table, and the gentle tinkle of the bell over the door. And after the bell — silence. Long silence.

Edgar offered one open eye to the scene and received nothing in reply. He opened the other eye and slowly raised his head to scan the room.

"Hello?"

Nothing. He was alone. The coffee urn burbled and the radiator, silent 'til now, heaved a hot sigh of relief.

A move to the window revealed nothing more to Edgar. The street was busier now, and blank corporate faces occasionally turned in to repay his vacant stare. All appeared normal; all appeared calm; in a blink the world appeared once again to have dropped into its greased grooves of mundane predestination.

Edgar gathered the money the man had left on the table to cover his meal, including a small tip within the prescribed percentages. He moved to the coffee urn and piddled a stream of coffee into his stained mug, sat back behind the counter, and sipped the slightly caustic liquid. After a moment, he began to flip through the morning tabloid, sitting where he always sat, doing what he always did at this time, day-in and day-out, for the last twenty-three years, contently oblivious to the logical conclusion that shortly, somewhere much closer to the river, a Mr. Wells would be meeting his maker slightly sooner than either he or his wife's insurance company had reckoned.

STOP ME IF YOU'VE HEARD THIS ONE

"A guy walks into a bar . . ."

It wasn't that the joke was funny or that I loved this man so very much, it was the way he threw himself into the telling. The way his face lit up, his eyes widened, his energy grew.

"A guy walks into a psychiatrist's office . . ."

How did it start, this ritual of ours? Does anyone know how rituals start? Robert knew I was stuck in the apartment all day. No, not stuck. Little Maggie was no trouble really, and maybe that was the point. A troublesome baby keeps you busy at least, walking them about, feeding, changing, singing tuneless songs in the key of their crying, praying for them to sleep. Maggie slept well without my prayers — so well that after playing with her, feeding her, setting her down for her nap, the household chores didn't really fill my day up. House? Third floor walk-up, one bedroom, kitchen off the living room. Five hundred square feet to sweep. A kitchen table to clear. An end table and bookshelf to dust. There was laundry to do and the supper to make — but always I could feel time expanding as it slowed, as my life tried to ease through the transition from a free girl to a married woman.

"A priest, a rabbi, and a politician are flying over the ocean . . ."

Robert would hear these jokes during the day — from his friends or colleagues at coffee or after class — and he would save them up for me. I would hear him running up the stairs. It didn't matter what kind of day he'd had, he would always run up the stairs to the apartment. I can still hear that sound — I would still know him by the cadence of his bounding steps on the stairs — the rhythm of them, how they lifted me from my day.

"A skeleton walks into a bar and orders a drink . . ."

Once in the door, he would kiss me, kiss the baby, then sit me down in the armchair. He'd take off his jacket, roll up the sleeves of his white shirt, loosen his narrow black tie — as if preparing for some heavy lifting — as if he'd shed the outside world, tossing it on the chair with his jacket. Then he'd unwrap the joke like a candy — offer it up like a present — to cheer up my day — to begin our evening together with laughter.

"A horse walks into a bar . . ."

And his joy in the telling — even though he already knew the joke — had practiced it to get it just right, rehearsing it during the long bus ride home — mouthing it, I'd always imagined, until the other riders looked away or watched with bemusement his animated reflection in the bus window. He'd savour it with me, smiling as he brought the ingredients together — set it up — added gestures or absurd expressions — a flourish of his hand, a broad accent. And he'd laugh with me, like a child — as if the joke were new — fresh to him as well. He made me feel that he felt my joy — shared my joy in his small gift.

"A duck walks into a hardware store . . ."

And sometimes he held Maggie in his arms as he told the joke — making faces and voices until she, too, was drunk with giggles.

"Teach me how to tell a joke," I'd say sometimes — to prolong the moment, to draw out his smile of mock exasperation. Then he would become a pompous professor, or a wizened guru, or maybe take on the loose swagger of a Borscht Belt comic. "There was a way to tell a joke," he explained. "First, you've got to stand up. No joke had ever been told properly sitting down."

"Why?" I'd ask.

"I don't know. It's just physics." And he'd wink his engineer eyes at me. And we'd switch spots — me standing, he in the chair with Maggie on his lap, and I'd stumble through a telling.

"A man walks into a patent office . . ."

"Whoa. Whoa! A man? A *guy* walks into a patent office."

"Why a 'guy,'" I'd asked?

"Easy," he replied. "Say 'man' and they'll want to know is he tall or short, skinny or fat, old or young. You're not giving evidence; you're telling a joke. Say 'guy' and everyone knows what you mean. A guy is just a guy."

This was just after we were married. 1951. We were living in that little third floor apartment on King near Ellice. Robert was in his last year of engineering. We lived off the money he made surveying in the summer, and the little the Navy paid after the war for servicemen to go to college, and the few dollars he got for helping professors with labs or tutoring a first-year student, and what my parents would sneak me after a supper at their place. We paid our bills. We made ends meet. But some months were so long.

"A bum asks a man for two dollars for a cup of coffee . . ."

I'd been working as a teller at the Royal Bank, but I became pregnant with our first — with Maggie. In those days there was no maternity leave. It wasn't even a question of working on until the last month. As soon as you knew, you told. And as soon as you told — well — one can't be so unseemly as to embarrass the clients or risk a mishap.

"A woman walks into a bank and asks to borrow two thousand dollars . . ."

We had other rituals. Rituals. That makes our life sound as if it were rigid and ordered. Certainties, maybe — as slight as they were — that made us feel we had some small control over our tiny moments in a world that was too big for us.

"A guy finds this bottle washed up on the beach . . ."

So many times we'd be down to our last dollar at the end of the week. Our supper would be fried bologna and ginger snaps. But each Saturday, we'd find a nickel, leave little Maggie with Mrs. Kurbis upstairs, walk down to the Dutch Maid ice cream shop on Osborne, buy a single vanilla cone, and share it on the walk back through the neighbourhood — King and Queen of all we surveyed.

"A guy walks into a tailor shop . . ."

Or if we found ourselves two or three dollars ahead, we'd ride downtown on the streetcar to the big stores (it seems a dream that we had streetcars back then, to look at the streets today) — buy a new white shirt for Robert — because white was what men wore back then — or maybe a scarf for me in anticipation of the coming cold — have a cup of coffee in the Eaton's cafeteria on the fifth floor — share a sweet pastry, maybe. Robert had a sweet tooth.

"A penguin takes his car to the garage . . ."

I remember the cold, reaching under our warped window frame each night as we held each other in bed. Sometimes we'd bring Maggie to our bed, bundle her between us, looking over her at each other. Whisper dreams into the darkness.

"A seal walks into a club . . ."

The innocence. The stupid, sweet innocence. The presumed naïveté of another time. The photographs. So few. Curled edges. No names on the back — relying too much on just knowing — until even that begins to slip away, to curl at the edges. Lives kept in a shoebox.

"Two friends were out hunting when one got bitten by a snake . . ."

When I'm gone too, will they find my shoebox — Maggie and Gordon? Will they find the diaries — read of our walks in the woods near the farm before we were married? So innocent. An unchaperoned kiss. Or the photo album he made for me after our trip to Grande Beach. His nickname for me — 'Flirt' — there in the margin in the careful print of a draftsman — the hint so pure and legible.

"A husband and wife are in the doctor's office . . ."

And he continued, when our life together finally grew big enough to challenge for its place in the larger world. When he moved up in his career — when the children grew — when the third-floor apartment became a two-story detached in the suburbs — when TV came to challenge for our attention — when age slowed his steps on the stairs and his walk became a shuffle, and his memory began to tear at the edges.

Still he would come home each day with a joke he'd collected. Despite the years, they were always new. After retirement, he would go out for coffee with his cronies — the 'senators' they called themselves — they in golf shirts; he still committed to his white shirt and jacket and tie. When they were done their expert analyses — when they'd solved the problems of the world and the neighbourhood, of the big leagues and the minors — he would offer them a last challenge: to provide one fresh joke, one new story to take home with him. And soon they were each competing here as well — vying to be the chosen one — the magi whose gift was carried back.

"An Englishman, a Scotsman, and an Irishman were about to face the firing squad . . ."

And what is he leaving me? What will his last gift be to his faithful audience, to his Sarah? As his grip on the world loosened, as he began to shred the past or recombine the pieces in his mind, recombining places, and names and dates, I began to doubt if my version were true. I reached a point where I tired of correcting him, lost the energy and surrendered. And so I began to lose my past along with him.

"This ninety-nine-year-old woman is brought before a judge for shoplifting . . ."

But I'll remember the way he'd reach out with one hand and touch my knee as he neared the punchline. How I'd explode with the joy of it, my hand wiping the tears from my eyes. Even to the end. Or will the end win? The remembrance of how blood looks on pavement. The crying sound of metal being prised apart. Night silence emphasized by the squawk of a radio. Flashing lights slicing the darkness on a highway. The smell of a hospital corridor, outside a room you don't want to enter.

"St. Peter watches a man pacing outside the pearly gates . . ."

His stupid, stupid jokes. This stupid, stupid man who has compelled me to sit here, holding his hand so tightly, going through his repertoire, giving him back the stories he had gifted me, surprising myself that I remember them all — laughing still at those curled punchlines. And I wish I could tell him. I wish he could speak. I wish he could smile to show that he knows how much I — how very much I — but he can't. My reward is the silence of the room, broken only by the rhythmic assurance of the machine at his bedside.

LIFE IN A BOTTLE

The ground was soft for digging and the sky was dark — no moon, but an occasional sweep of light from the traffic on the road high up at the top of the embankment.

That was the summer of the heavy rain. The rains that caused the spruce trees to explode with green pine cones that littered the ground like goose shit — the cones that smelled so good crushed in your hand — tossed in the boiled water — their sharp astringent taste keeping the hunger away a little longer.

Maybe it wasn't so bad as that. Amy handled it best. Every few weeks or so she'd take us to the university, where the research people would buy a pint of our blood. Cash — not much, but enough that pooled we could get a jug or two of beer in the campus pub. Being down a pint would make the buzz come faster and stay longer. But there were forms to sign — I don't like to make my name — give my name — to them — to anyone.

Even Amy didn't know my name — or if she did, she didn't use it. Love, she called me — 'Luv' it came out as, in her English accent — her soft accent — consonants littered or lost — like all the edges had worn away. And I didn't know anything about her — except her first name. I didn't ask. Two years we were together. I never asked. Or if she told me, I've forgotten. I've forgotten so many things, I think.

On the street it wasn't easy anymore to put the touch on someone. It was different when I was younger — before they changed the rules. You can't ask for money now. Now you can't touch anyone — can't even look them in the eye. Too aggressive, they say.

Before I'd just come up to some guy on the corner as he waited for the light to change. No escape. I'd come up — big, but friendly — drop my heavy hand on his shoulder — laugh loud — call him 'buddy,' like I know him — like I give a shit. And he'd throw some coins at me — to make me scramble — so he could get away. I'd just laugh — Yell "thanks, buddy!" — as cheerful as I could — at the retreating crowd he'd dissolved into — the crowd on my side of the street parting around me.

Now I'm too threatening. Not my size — people can deal with that. It's my face — the scars — my few yellow teeth, like fangs — the way my head jerks — twitches when I'm angry or hungry or tired — or when I hoard my meds to sell on the street — or when I can't be bothered to check in at the clinic regular like they want me to.

People back away now — like they'll catch something — like I'm breathing something into the air that they'll carry home to their family — that'll turn their kids into me.

Not a problem for Amy. She has this smile — that waif look that gets sympathy — that makes people think of a distant daughter or sister who just needs a few dollars to make it right. Her clothes aren't new, but they're not torn or dirty. She's careful with them. Soft tones with a splash of colour — like her voice — like a soft laugh. Most days she wears them high on the shoulder to cover the tattoos — hiding the swirls of artwork.

And she'll make our signs sometimes. They let you use signs — no speaking, but signs are okay. She'll find the cardboard flap from a box — take it into the library and borrow a marker and do the lettering. Not that I can't write — I can — but my hands are big and clumsy — my block letters look hard, like a shout. She has curves to her letters — adds a happy face or a butterfly — makes the message seem positive and real — draws the loose change from unsure hands — coins collecting in the empty Tim Hortons cup in front of us. The sign that says we're from out of town — we just need a few dollars to get back — to return home — leave the area — stop being a burden here — to become someone else's problem.

And when we've been too long on one corner — when they recognize us — when they can no longer be part of our lie — she'll put the cardboard down on the sidewalk — salt it with a few coins — start singing softly — folk songs and lullabies from her home — from when she was young. Her high, pure tones sound so sweet that I'll rest my head against the brick and sleep — dreamless for a change — float on her song — wake to see our small stack of coins grown to something that'll get us through another day or two.

Before the snow comes, we sleep in the woods by the river — in the protected land — where the bank down to the water is too steep for houses — the ground too unstable to build anything lasting. We have a lean-to I made from fallen trees and a tarp I took from someone's back yard — that had protected their expensive car from sun or rain or hail. Orange. Bright, like a toy — all tied together with yellow plastic cord. I know how to tie knots — make it secure — keep the wind from carrying it off.

The lean-to's okay, when the weather's warm — or when Amy and I are close together under the blanket — or when we've scored something to take the chill off. And the sound of rain is nice — like fingers tapping — like a ticking clock in a hallway.

When the snow comes — when the frost hardens the ground — when the frost turns my hair white and we wake in the morning, my knees stiff so I walk like an old man — then we try to move inside. But the shelters are no good. They split us up to different rooms — make us sleep on mats on the floor — so close you can smell the next guy — makes your sleep fitful — your dreams overlap with theirs. People steal your stuff. No respect. Animals. You have to leave early in the morning. You can't be drunk or high.

So we find somewhere — a building left open — a back window I can break without too much noise — a stairwell. But now there are so many cameras and alarms, and we have to watch the time. Get up early like a worker so we aren't caught. Gather our things and be gone before anyone sees us — move from spot to spot so we don't get too comfortable — get too lazy about it. Get caught and we get our asses kicked by the cops. Get angry — get angry and they kick you more.

I've worked. I've had jobs — when I was younger. I carried things, when I could. Stacked boxes in warehouses. Picked up trash. Painted fences and lamp poles. Was a soldier for a while. Or maybe I dreamed I was a soldier when I was a kid. But that's been painted over too.

I worked in a slaughterhouse when oil prices were high — when they'd take anyone. They gave me a bolt gun for 'knocking' the cattle — pressing it to their forehead and firing a bolt. Sometimes the cow would move at the last second and you'd miss — hit a vein — blood spirting out all over you — the sudden iron smell. The first cow of the day was okay, but once there's blood in the air — the other cows smell it — smell the fear — the kill floor stinks with the ammonia smell of piss. I lasted three days. Maybe it was the killing — or the need to be sober. Or maybe because I started to wonder about the feel of it against my forehead — the sudden release — seeing myself swaying on the hook above — peaceful.

And I cooked. I liked doing that. Someone taught me so
I'd have something to do when I got out — to keep me out —
something for me. Now — over an open fire — using an old coffee
can — I'll make Amy and me tea sweetened with the sugar and
cream we take from the outdoor tables — can't go inside anymore.
Or use the pine cones I've scooped from the ground and stuffed into
my pockets. Stew, sometimes — or soup — if we have a little extra
for a can of this or that.

People will give us stuff too — if they're not okay tossing
coins in the hat — not okay us using the money how we want or
need — not how they think we should. Sometimes people will
toss sandwiches on our cardboard — the half they didn't want.
Sometimes they're wrapped tight, like they brought it special from
home — thought special of us when they made their own lunch that
morning. Those are good.

One guy said he wouldn't give me money, but he'd take me to a
place for soup or coffee — so he'd know how his money was spent.

I pushed him — when he tried to touch my arm — when he
tried to lead me — take my arm like a child or an idiot. Pushed him
into a wall — not hard — but too hard. I'm too big. He fell. Staggered
up. People came — a half circle of them with me against the wall
— the smear of blood on the brick. We had to go — Amy and me —
find another corner to sit on — another wall to rest against.

Then came the night when we were sleeping in the woods. I
woke on my back to the smell of something burning — like the
woods were on fire — the stars above exploding like fireworks — the
sky all quick short bursts. I tried to wake Amy for her to see, but my
words were mumbled and when she finally woke she stared at me. I
tried to point to the sky. But my arm wouldn't move from my side.

Some of its use came back — slowly — but I push my right
hand in my pocket now so it doesn't seem obvious. And my speech
came back — mostly — enough that Amy can understand me.
But some sounds I can't make. Some letters. My name. Now I
mispronounce myself.

Sometimes Amy and me we eat at the soup kitchen — when it's
cold or we're really hungry. Get the beef and potatoes and gravy and
soft vegetables. I don't like the look of the servers, though — the
volunteers — who give you an extra scoop of this or that and a sly

wink like they make all the difference — like it's all about how good they are — to be volunteering — to be helping someone like me.

I hear them, as I move down the line — heads nodding in my direction — "look at him" — "poor guy" — "if only" this or that — like they know my story — like they know who I am — like their measured scoops make a fuck of a difference to me. Like a second dessert will save me. Fatten me up for Jesus. Like I'm their sacrifice that'll get them closer to their god — buy their own salvation.

I take the food. I fill my stomach against the cold — against the hollow week. But afterwards — I'll go out to the parking lot — squat on a car — shit on a car — just to show them.

Amy doesn't like that — cries sometimes — says we need them. And I feel bad. But I don't think they notice — notice even that — cause next week we're back — them still smiling — still the wink like they maybe know, but they don't. Like I'm supposed to say something.

Sometimes I start to shake so bad the tray spills — the fork and knife hit the floor at my feet with a broken bell sound — and Amy has to take me to a table to sit down. And she'll stand there — hold me until the shaking stops and I can eat — stand behind me, her arms reaching up to drape over my big, useless frame. Or she'll sit on my knee — feed me — wipe the gravy from my chin with the thin paper napkin — scraping the pudding from the side of my mouth with a spoon as I clutch my elbows trying to keep everything from spilling out.

But the servers, they won't come over then. As I shake, they disappear. Suddenly there's something they need to do in the kitchen — out of sight.

I used to catch birds. Small birds. Sparrows. Chickadees. Cedar Waxwings. Amy knew all the names. Nothing cruel. I just noticed in the fall that they liked to eat the berries on a certain kind of tree — red berries that had passed ripe — started to ferment on the branch. They'd get drunk, these birds, and fly all crazy-like — flop on the ground — too stoned to fly. So I'd pick those berries — all I could find — and place them on the ground. Hide back in the bushes or around the corner — protect the area from cats and the like — wait until the birds were good and drunk and then go and pick them up. Gentle. Put them in an old shoe box. Walk with my box of drunken birds to a guy I knew. I don't know what he did with them — pets maybe or pet food. Food for a snake. I only know I got twenty-five cents each.

Amy never liked it when I caught birds. She thought it was mean. So I told her the guy had a pet store — that he sold the birds to families — so the birds would live inside with food and water — protected from anything that would prey on them. I told her they would sing — teach children how to whistle. She liked that. That settled her — calmed her. I could do that — calm her. Talk to her. Maybe that was my purpose — between the shaking and the bullshit — my sudden anger. To give Amy someone to care for — someone worse off than she was.

And she would always keep one bird — pick it up from the ground — cradle it until the berries wore off and it could fly again.

Now the ground was soft again for digging, so I could make the sides of the hole smooth — the corners sharp — using the shovel we took from the city truck when the crew went around the corner for a smoke. I can do good work when I want to. I can take pride in what I do. At least I used to, I think.

I kept the hole shallow, though. No more than waist deep on me — although that's plenty deep on Amy. Anything deeper is a waste. Unnecessary. Stupid. A holdover — from what and where and why I don't know and can't remember.

As I dug, Amy sat a few yards away, her back against a tree. The bird in her hands began to twitch — roll over — one wing waking up faster than the other — sporadic efforts that made it dance around on the platform she made of her open hands — palms upward — like an offering — level with her chin so she could watch over it — judge when it was ready.

Just as I was finishing — just as I drove the shovel into the pile of waste dirt at the top — the bird seemed to recover and flew to a perch several feet up. Amy stood. For a moment they were eye level — she still, it twitching and darting. Finally, it was gone. She turned back. Me standing in the hole — we were eye to eye now, me and Amy.

"Time?" she asked — no expression in her voice, but tired, I thought.

I nodded. Lay down at the bottom of the hole. Full length. Restful. Crossed my arms over my chest.

"You never sleep like that," she said.

"You can rest the bottle under my hands. That will protect it. When you start shovelling the earth in. There aren't any rocks — but a clump might break it — break the bottle."

She shook her head — muttered something, looking at the shovel.

I'd gotten tired, that's all — can't take care of myself — shake all the time. I can't take care of Amy. I'm slow. Hurt all the time. Some days I can't stand straight. I'm a danger to her. She's taking care of me — it's a waste of her time — her energy. She could do better without me. I'm too big. I scare people away. She could always do better with a smile — without me in the shadows — arms crossed, rocking on my feet, trying to keep warm — never warm anymore, even in the summer — trying to keep away — in the shadows — trying not to be seen or to be obvious.

So I told her. Had her write this out so you'd know. If you found me.

You see, it's got to be clear — if I'm found — if I'm ever found — that nothing happened. Amy's not responsible. It was my idea.

I said for her to drive the shovel into my neck. I asked her. I showed her where. Scratched a line on my neck with my nail. Even took a rock and ran it over the edge of the shovel blade to sharpen it. But she knew it would take two, maybe three blows — knew that the first would be the hardest, but once I was hurt — once I was bleeding — twitching like one of her birds maybe — me bleeding out like I was smeared with berries. She knew her heart would tell her that she had to hit me again — and maybe again — that it would be kindest — that it would make my pain go away. Then she'd cover me up with the dirt — as I bled out — it was all how I asked her to do it. She's strong. Steady. Not like me.

It's what I wanted — to die like that — like — like a soldier — like a knight or something — something I thought I remembered from stories I read as a boy. Or saw in a play. Adventure stories. Heroes. Quests. Purpose.

But I looked at her — into her eyes — saw how wet they were — saw for maybe the first time in my big, stupid life what I did to someone else. That it would hurt her. So I reached into my pocket and took the pills — the medication I'd been hoarding over the months — the stuff they'd give me at the clinic — never thinking to ask why I was showing up regular for a change — after so long.

I took all the pills — washed them down — emptied the bottle — this bottle. Choked back the vomit — the fight.

She touched the handle of the shovel — walked past it — slid down into the hole. Knelt by me. She took the bottle from me — the empty bottle — promised to roll up this story — our story — write down the story I'm telling in her round kind letters — place it inside. For if I'm ever found.

In my dreams, she puts the bottle under my hands. Presses her hands against mine. Kneels next to me — looking down on me. Kisses my forehead.

Then rests her tiny head on my chest — like it was any other night — waits for me to calm — waits for me to sleep.

PENNIES IN A JAR

I was surprised when it was the bone tumour in his upper arm that took him. It wasn't supposed to be that. It was supposed to be one of the tumours in his brain — one of the tumours that had sent him to the hospital in the first place — the tumours that had secretly grown to the point that they pushed against some nerve or some pocket of cells and caused him to fall one morning — to wake from the deconstruction of sleep to find that his vision was blurred — that he had no balance — that his speech was a jumble of sounds, slippery to his grasp. The tumours that left him unable to call for help from the floor. And he remained on the floor for almost three days until I came by to find out why he hadn't returned any of my calls — irate that he'd missed our lunch appointment — an appointment he'd insisted upon to discuss something he'd thought was important. The bone tumour wasn't supposed to do it. It was just supposed to be one of those add-ons that cancer is so fond of.

Initially the chemotherapy had helped. The steroids had reduced the size of the brain tumours, restoring most of his vision, returning some of his balance, providing a degree of traction to his thoughts. If you ignored the hospital smell, the paleness of the light in the room, the insistent calmness of the paint colour and the metronomic beep of machines, the plastic bags of liquids, his body punctured with tubes dripping so many earth tones into or from the pallor of his body, the skin yellow like the pages of an old book, the wisps of hair like fungus on his peeling scalp — if you could ignore all that you could convince yourself that everything was normal, that all would be well.

It was April, two years ago now. The snow was still in the shadows, but the chill in the open air was fast giving way to spring. It should have been a time of hope.

"The ground will be soft soon."

Ben startled me from my own stupor. I was sitting in the green faux-leather chair by his bed, scrolling through my phone to reread articles I didn't remember reading minutes ago. He'd been sedated against the pain and hadn't spoken for coming on a day and a half.

"Ben. It's me, Richard. I'm here."

"The ground. It'll be time for digging soon."

He hadn't turned to me or acknowledged my voice. His eyes were still closed. His head was tilted back on the thin pillow. His voice was raspy, scratched by the procedures or burned by the drugs, or brittle from lack of use.

"Digging? Ben? What digging?"

"The coins."

"What coins? Ben? Ben?"

But he was gone again, lost beneath the waves. The only reply was the whir of the morphine pump.

This was early in the month, before he took the final turn, before the drugs fell behind, before the full vigil began. Before we — our older sister Liz and I — would take turns, sitting shifts so someone would always be there — so he wouldn't die alone.

But I'm getting ahead of myself. That would happen in due time. We had two weeks yet, though we didn't know it. This, as I said, was still early in the month, when everything was still informal, when I could still pretend that showing up would do any good. Then, commensurate with his condition at the time, Liz and I visited for short stretches each, with a little overlap, covering only the day. The night was still for sleep in our own beds.

When Liz arrived an hour or so later, I asked about the digging, the coins. She didn't know. Babbling, she suggested. The drugs.

The next morning I arrived a little late, after Liz has gone home to check on her kids. They were old enough to take care of themselves, I thought — at least for a handful of hours in the morning — but she knew better. She insisted on a schedule for them, on limits, on boundaries.

A tea in one hand, a muffin in a bag in the other, I fumbled with my coat. Ben was sitting up in bed. One of the good days. This was still a time of unreasonable hope.

"You bring one for me?" His voice was clear and solid. I paused for a moment before tossing my coat onto the chair.

"Take mine," I offered.

"You sure?"

"I already had one at the house."

I placed the cup on the tray. He nodded a thanks but waved away the muffin.

"No solids," he reminded.

I watched as his hands removed the plastic lid on the reddish-brown cardboard cup with only a trace of the shakes.

"Cream? Two sugars?" he asked.

"Of course. Same as you like. We're twins, after all."

A fatuous comment, I thought as I watched him. He used both hands to bring the cup to his lips: his right wrist showing the hospital bracelet, the left trailing the tube taped just below the elbow. We were twins only in the coincidence of birth — in some shared statistics — a similarity in the bones of our face, our colouring. Beyond that —

"Good. Good." he proclaimed. "Better than the tepid crap they bring around here. Usually at two in the morning. 'Wake up, we brought tea,' they proclaim, like they'd just split the atom. Or cured cancer."

He'd lowered the cup, watching it with a worried look that stood in contrast with the flippancy of his speech. I took it from his hands and placed it on the table to the side of the bed.

"It's here when you need it. Let me know when you're ready."

We are not twins — were not twins. Not true twins. A rough resemblance, nothing more: the hair, around the eyes, I'd been told. He was bigger. More physical. That may have been the years as a surveyor: summers outdoors, the activity. More nature than nurture. But that was melting away now. Some of my thinness was now showing through on him.

"Have you been —?" he nodded vaguely in my direction, through me to the green chair.

"No. Not all the time. Liz has been here, too. And there was a visitor."

"I'd wake sometimes, see you there. Wake again, see Liz. Then the next time it was one of the guys from — from —"

"Work. Sam. Yes. I think he said Sam. One of your contractor clients."

"It was like I'd blink and the person in the chair would disappear — morph into someone else."

"It's a magic chair. It must be for what the room costs."

This caught him in mid-thought. I could do that sometimes. His head clicked over to me. He smiled. No need to talk about the extra cost for the private room. His lack of insurance. I didn't begrudge him this. No need to bring it up.

"How's the pain?" I asked.

"Fine."

"A five? Seven?"

"Fine. Five, maybe."

"Do you need —?" He was allowed an extra shot of morphine every few hours, but he had to ask. I fumbled with the cord that had the call button to get the nurse, pulling it clear from where it had become hidden by the sheets and the metal rail at the side of the bed, holding it up for him to see. "Do you want —?"

"No. Not yet. I want to be clear. This has been too sudden. There are some things — some arrangements —"

"The coins?"

Again I'd caught him. This time he looked me in the eyes. I saw how the blue in his was cloudy now, not like it had been when we were boys, when we were growing up. Not bright like then.

"There's something I need you to do for me."

"Anything."

And then he told me. At first it didn't make sense.

He was a surveyor, my brother. He measured ground. He placed stakes so the machine operators would know where to move dirt: how deep to cut — how much to fill. He placed iron pins that set official limits — established legal demarcations between lots. He helped build new developments where people would live.

"My place — my house — I decided to move into that neighbourhood when it was just finished. Got a deal from the developer. How long ago was that? Forty years?"

"That you've lived in that house? At least."

"Mine was one of the first. I'd done the original survey. Done all the construction layout for the pipes and the streets and the grading. I was sad about the work, sometimes. The area had been a beautiful place before the development. Magical. Large trees, hidden groves — a place a child could spend all summer exploring. It reminded me of where we grew up."

"Back east? Balmoral?"

"Yeah. That little house just on the edge of town. You and I, we could walk out our backyard into forests and down to creeks to catch frogs. It was always adventures."

"That was you — the adventures. I was only out there when I was sent to find you. When you were late for supper."

"Days spent running free. Magic."

"Well, it's gone now. All developed. Subdivisions and industrial parks all the way to the highway. Progress."

Shortly after moving in, he said, he decided that his new place should be magical as well. He was making decent money then — had been working for years, since our own father had kicked him out. He remembered the magic of wandering the forests searching for adventure, for treasure.

"The new development was a barren place. All the trees were gone. Streets replaced the paths. The creeks were buried — contained in pipes underground."

"So? It's what you did, or helped to do."

"Yes. It was." He paused for a moment, his mouth slack. "So I decided to grow my own magic if none existed. I decided to bury coins in the ground."

"You buried coins?"

"Not directly, no. Not individually. I filled mason jars with coins — small coins: pennies, nickels, a few dimes, fewer quarters, maybe a silver dollar — sometimes a foreign coin or two."

"Mason jars full of pennies?"

"This was back then. It wasn't meant to be much, but treasure to a child. Not always a mason jar. Sometimes I'd pick up an earthenware jar at a flea market for a few dollars."

"Jars? How many?"

"So far? Maybe a hundred, a hundred and fifty. I'd have to check my map."

"You buried a hundred and fifty jars of coins?"

"Not all at once. I knew where all the property lines were — where the houses would be set back from the road — which areas were safe. So, I buried them all. Not deep. A foot or two — never more. Before the houses were built, before people moved in. They're all in place, waiting to be found — to be discovered."

He had put out the stakes — the final grades. He knew where the ground would be shaved down or where two or three feet of fill would be placed. He did the initial survey and the final survey — to check the grades — to measure the amount of dirt moved to pay the contractor.

"Later, I'd plant a map at a house that I saw had a child living there — maybe a child that I saw looking bored in the antiseptic suburbia they'd been transplanted into.

"Plant?"

"Hide. I couldn't mail it or anything. That would be too creepy. You have to be careful. Especially nowadays. People assume. An old man. Children. People assume."

"No kidding."

"And the maps couldn't be given; they had to be found. Discovery. That's part of the magic."

He was reaching for the tea. I placed it on the tray again, within reach, then sat in the chair, picking raisins from my muffin. He'd take a late-night stroll with his dog, he said — what was the dog's name — the one that died a few years back?

"Ranger. He legitimized the walk — added a sort of innocence — allowed a proximity to fences or yards. If anyone saw me, it was always, *bad dog. What are you doing there?*"

He'd place the map somewhere where the child would see it.

As well as being a surveyor, he was a draftsman. You had to be in his day, before computers. He drew the maps that arose from the survey, using pots of ink and metal scribes to put the lines and contours on the linen paper.

"I'd find old, yellowed paper around the office, or age the printing paper they used in the old days to make blueprint copies of plans — leaving it out in the air to let the ammonia set. Then heat it, to brown it irregularly, crimp the edges."

And he'd place it where a kid would find it — in the loose dirt beside a sandbox, behind a shed where bikes were kept when it rained. He knew kids — knew this would be a secret — something they'd hold close to themselves. They would go out, with their plastic tools or borrowed shovels twice their height, and find the treasure the map revealed to them — the treasure that had been waiting for them sometimes since twenty years before they were born.

"Go back to my place. In the roll-top desk — the one our grandfather made. You'll find a cardboard tube. Inside. Look inside it."

"And I'll find the map?"

"The master, yes, with all the locations shown. I make smaller versions — specific to each treasure — specific to one spot that would be theirs. I didn't send all the maps out at once. I've spread them out over the years. I wanted the neighbourhood to develop a mystery. New kids coming in would hear stories from the older kids — maybe the older kids are now parents themselves, staying in the family home or buying on a nearby street."

"Why?"

"Don't you remember being a child, Richard? Adults knew everything. They owned our world. They used that voice — those sharp-edged tones of assurance — to cut through the fear of the dark or the unknown, until there was nothing left — making sense of things, but taking the sense of wonder with it. But as a child you don't realize that inside the adult is their child form that never changes, never loses the same fears — never really controls anything of importance in the bigger world. If children knew that, the world would collapse on itself. Only as you grow older do you realize that you're responsible for the careful juggling — how close the balance is to collapse — how important it is to give a child a small piece of the world that they can hold in their hands."

"What are you, Peter Pan — trying never to grow up?"

"Peter Pan isn't about never growing up. It's about death. It's about the lost boys — lost even in the middle of Pan's story."

He tapped his finger against the side of the cardboard cup.

"So, what am I supposed to do with this map?'

"I need you — I want you to finish for me. I've got — what — maybe twenty more spots to be found? The map will show the ones I've let be discovered — red checks next to them. The others are still waiting. The map has hundreds of Xs — they mark the spot. One a year — maybe two — never more or it'd kill the magic. Can you do it for me?"

"Why me? Why not Liz? She's older. She had kids."

"Because you understand. Because who best to finish a life's work than a twin?"

He was tired now. I could tell. Exhausted — from the effort, from the pain. As if he knew. A man who had travelled the world who knew that this room — the green painted walls with the cheap framed pictures of fields and sunrises — would be the last representation of the world he would ever see.

He'd started to lift the tea again, but had thought better of it — had known it would not end well. His head fell back on the pillow; his eyes closed; his hands reflexively clutched and released the edges of his paper gown. Then he was still. His breathing began a rhythmic rattle. I moved the cup and tray to one side. Sat back in the chair.

I don't miss my childhood, but I miss the way I took pleasure in small things. I couldn't control the world I was in, but I was able to find joy in the things that made me happy: an afternoon in my room playing with toy soldiers, reading my books on science in the moving shade beneath our bedroom window — trying to put order and safety and control into a world that I knew, with growing certainty, had none. For Ben the joy was poking sticks into the mud of the stream flats, or whistling tunes as he scanned the trees for nests of speckled eggs. I preferred to discover the world through pictures and diagrams.

He never married, my brother. Neither did I. No reason. I could just never see myself that connected to another — couldn't understand letting someone else inside to know me where I didn't know myself. For Ben, it was because he never stopped moving long enough, could never find someone who could keep up.

When he became a surveyor, it was for necessity — for survival. In the summers he'd work the long hours, sometimes in foreign countries, to bring enough money back to make it through the winter. He saw the world, much of it through the lens of a level.

Late in the year, when the local cold and the frozen ground stopped construction and seized the instruments, he returned to his small home to be a writer. He could have returned to those foreign countries, but instead he'd set a fire in the fireplace, take down one of the bottles of scotch he'd retrieved during his travels, lock the door against the world. There he'd steal the observed events of other's lives to fill in the gaps of his own — measuring the cuts and fills, reshaping the landscape. Stories mostly, and poems. He was published now and then, in periodicals. I have the magazines somewhere, but I doubt if he ever made enough to pay for the ink.

His house was small — the smallest in the development. A tiny two-story, with a kitchen and living room on the ground floor and two bedrooms upstairs. One he used for an office — for his survey work, for his writing hobby. It was the smallest, facing north, slanting ceilings beneath a dormer. A drafting table stood against one wall, with a desk beneath the window. A small ledge ran outside the window, barely the width of a book. Once he told me how he would put his glass of scotch on the window sill to catch the first spring rain of the city — not for its purity, but for the soot that "added smokiness to the scotch." Not being a drinker, I didn't know if he was lying to me. It sounded like his style of truth.

That he would waste his money infuriated me. That he worked only half the year, draining down his savings during the other half, putting what little he had left in jars to bury in the dirt to sit for decades for children to find them. Perhaps they were the coins he made from his writing.

We weren't close, my brother and I. Just because we're twins doesn't mean that. Perhaps our confined time together spent our limited tolerance for each other. We were as close as brothers sometimes are nowadays — calls on holidays, the occasional lunch — but we shared little. There was no point, no incident, that marked our separation but the biological milestone. The splitting of our cells *in utero* was effective and efficient and permanent.

He left home when our father challenged him — left to find his way. I did too, but not out of solidarity — that wasn't how I thought things through. Mother had been dead three years by then. Whether it changed our father, hardening him or removing the buffer that cushioned us from his version of the world, I can't say. I only know that the world crumbled a little, and Ben saw the light through the chinks. I only know that he left, and I followed. But he took a job, found his independence hidden in the clutter of his life — liked that the pieces of his world were loose, to be reassembled at a whim at his choosing. But when my money ran out, I returned to become the son again, the child. I returned to school, took my degree. But then I was never a target.

Parents are supposed to love their children equally. How do you choose one over the other? How do you select a twin? The month before I graduated, father died — an accident — a slip on the pavement while crossing a busy road. So simple. No lingering. The family house, now surrounded by newer homes, was sold. Liz was married only a few months then and needed her share of the money for her new life. The new owner tore the house down, combined the lot with another, built apartments. Urban renewal. In-fill.

You can't see the future man within the child. There's no treasure buried there. A man, as he grows, makes choices based upon the experiences of the child. He only realizes later that the childhood assumptions — about adult infallibility, about world certainties — are all false. After living under the eyes of our parent gods, with a promise of divinity, the realization that you are a mortal man is a pain from which we never recover.

But now Ben is gone. When I went to his house, with Liz, to attend to his things — to clean out the place to get ready for the sale — it was odd, piercingly so, to walk into his home, to find it as it was when he was felled. The rusted house plants. A book open on a table — a novel, I was surprised to see, by a Russian no one's read for decades. A coffee cup next to it, the coffee gone now but with a dark brown ring extending down an inch or so below the lip, like a scar.

In his bedroom office was the roll top desk. Small, in a dark walnut stain. It was open. A bottle of ink was open as well, a blue film dried in the bottom, like a bruise. Next to it was a scribe: a short wooden shaft, five or six inches long, with a stainless-steel nib on the end. It too had a blue, crusted stain where the ink was meant to flow down. He'd been working when he fell, perhaps just finishing — caught in the act of cleaning up.

The edge of the Persian carpet in the hallway was rolled back, likely by the medics I'd called — I couldn't remember — for it was here in the hallway that I'd found him. A picture on the wall was crooked, knocked at some point. As I straightened it, I saw it was an oil, original, a foreign scene in spring. There was a stain on the hardwood floor, evidence of the time he'd spent there immobile until I came. Part of me felt a shame, a regret, that I had not come back to rearrange, to clean, after I'd seen him to the hospital. That I'd left the evidence of his fall. Perhaps if I'd believed in his return.

In the desk I found the cardboard tube. I didn't tell Liz. She asked if I wanted the desk, for my office. She knows my weakness for antiques. Weeks later it was in my house, in my den. It was only then that I opened the tube, slid out the paper, unrolled it on the hardwood floor, used books to hold down the edges while I took it in.

It was not large, really, for what it contained — perhaps three feet by four. On it were the crisp lines of a legal survey plan: angles clear and delineated, the lots numbered and sized. And there were small Xs, hundreds of them, like a pirate map gone mad, some with small red checks next to them. But no pirate would have located their treasures so precisely — distances double-referenced to property corners, depths of bury noted, decimal measurements to hundredths of a foot.

In the corner was a date — when he had started all this — so long ago that I was surprised that someone as young as that would have gone to so much trouble, had so much foresight. I sat for a minute wondering what had occupied my own mind while he was busy salting a new subdivision with childlike treasure that would not, as was now a fact, be recovered in his lifetime.

Inside as well were smaller papers: yellowed, single sheets. Most were blank. One looked complete — a window of the main map reproduced, but at a larger scale. But here the lines were not as accurate but wide, bold sweeps. The writing was less precise, too, a more cursive, flowing, script — as if done by a pirate with a quill pen on a rolling sea after too much rum. There was a north arrow — an N crowning an eagle, of all things, whose outstretched wings encompassed east and west, his taloned claws clutching south. The X was crude and large, but the location was precise. There could be no mistake. I could find this house, this prize, easily.

Another map was partially complete. The lot and street were in place, and the X, but there was no writing yet, no north arrow, and there were none of the symbols that marked trees — the kind of detail that brought the map to life, that pulled it forward to the present day. So small, these maps, but giant in the hands of a child. Even small maps can contain a world.

When I'd first gathered his things, placing books and papers in a leather bag I'd found slung over his chair — when I'd left his house, his small house, I'd turned left, away from my car, to walk through the streets of this 'magical' place. The houses were no different than those that surrounded me where I lived. The streets were lined with the same cars and trucks and SUVs. I returned through the alley, where he'd walked his dog on those clandestine nights. His compact house, painted dark blue, stood on the same sized lots as the others. But with the space he'd gained, he'd made a garden in his backyard. Not a garden, for the flowers were wildflowers, left to find their own patterns. The trees were not trimmed, but seemed to choose for themselves what to shade and what to leave bare. And through the yard wound a path. It was made of bricks placed in a herringbone pattern — old bricks of a colour and type you don't see anymore. His work took him to sites that were to be demolished to make way for change. He must have salvaged as many as he could carry back to his truck, placing them down on the rough soil, nurturing moss to fill the cracks between them.

As I stood on this path, I could hear the neighbourhood sound of young children — the definitive cries of childhood logic that formed a game out of chaos and secret rules.

Is magic an antique, I wondered as my eye followed the sweep of the path to his backdoor. Maybe it's a casualty of progress — the detailed nature of technology smothering it. Magic requires the edges of science to remain blurred.

The house would fetch a good price, more for the lot than the house, which would probably be razed, the garden paved over, the path removed.

I remembered reading once that to be young, to be a child, is to see the world as new. To be an adult, to reach maturity, is to know that the world is broken. To be old, to know that all is lost and death is near, is to know that the world will never be fixed.

Ben was cremated, according to his wishes. Liz and I split his ashes. Hers are in a copper and steel urn on the mantel of her living room fireplace. Mine I put in an earthenware jar, with a handful of small coins, and buried in the garden of my backyard, a salvaged brick the only headstone.

Maybe we were twins. Lately, I feel the morning ache in my bones. The dreams I wake from in the early hours are too often of something growing inside of me, choking life from me — of death rampant inside me clawing to get out — the certainty that my abilities are waning. Do Ben and I share our defects the way we shared the colour of our eyes or the shape of our chins or our quickness to find the harmony in a tune on the radio?

It was only several weeks later that I sat one night at the desk, and dipped the steel stylus into the pot of India ink to make the first tentative strokes on the yellowed paper, joining my lines to my brother's on an unfinished map.

CHANCE ENCOUNTER

Outside, the late fall scene was playing out as the wind chased the leaves from cover to cover, tossing gravel up in swirls to scratch at the window. She turned slowly back with a tired shrug to the room and caught the stare of the man three tables down. God, not again. He looked away quickly, feigning interest in the container of sugar packets on his table, then in the waitress wiping down the counter, then the grey man at a far table nursing a beer. She turned away, too, as she had been taught, looking down at her coffee cup as if the answers to the questions of the universe would soon come floating to its tepid surface.

A boy, she thought. A bird not long from the nest, testing his range. Then a smile began to grow on her face, and she looked up slowly — directly — and met his gaze. And this time he didn't turn away, but found a smile of his own to match hers.

He wasn't handsome, she saw now — now that she allowed herself the luxury to observe. But his face had a pleasing imbalance to it, as if God were playing a kind of joke in the way that the various pieces didn't seem to go together: the slightly longish nose, the large eyes, the crooked grin, the angular bones — like strangers forced to stand together in a shelter until the next bus arrived.

An impasse now? Smiles exchanged, they were too far apart to have any kind of conversation, to communicate in any depth. She touched tentatively a strand of hair and tilted her head down in a shy look, but he looked down again, and she felt a small sadness that her attempt at action would now fizzle and die. 'Boldness we hardly knew ye.'

He stood as if to go, grabbing his jacket from the back of the chair and dropping some heavy coins on the table, but then moved towards her in measured steps. He wore a denim shirt, pale over a dark T-shirt, that hung in comfortable folds on a frame one size too tall and two sizes too narrow. The jacket, held in his hand like a piece of rope or a vacant leash, was a thin, dark blue wind breaker.

"I, uh — I —" he began, his gaze floating up with the words.

"— couldn't help noticing me?"

"Yes. I saw you —"

"— looking."

"— and I thought —"

"— you'd come over and say hi."

"Yes. You have a lovely smile."

"Yes. I do."

He cocked his head to one side and gave her a look which could have been bemusement or else confusion — that he was no longer sure they spoke the same language — like when you give your dog the wrong command.

"Sit."

"Pardon?"

"You could sit and join me," she offered as a stick for him to chase.

"Yes. Thanks. Yes."

He tossed his jacket across the chair and sat opposite. He placed his hands on the table, left resting gently over the right. Nails and cuticles a little chewed, she noted. No wedding ring, just a steel ring on the small finger of his right hand, next to a gold signet ring — an odd design of interlocking angles and lines with the letter G in the middle.

"Garry?" she said.

"What?"

"Garry. With two Rs. Is that your name?"

"No. It's Donald — Don. And yours?"

"You have to guess."

He gave her a slightly sad look, like a student half way through an exam that's going badly.

"I'm not —"

"— very good at games? Go ahead. You're probably better than you think. I'll give you a hint."

She reached out with her index finger and touched his gold ring, tracing the sharp angle in the design that formed an unintended V shape.

"Gabrielle?"

"Right. And on the first guess, too," she added without hesitation. "Such luck. You must win all sorts of prizes."

He looked at her cockeyed again, then made a small smile.

"Some nights are luckier than others."

The waitress finally found her way to their table. He began to motion her away.

"I'd like a wine, actually," she interjected. "Dry red, if you have it."

"Sure. Anything for you?"

"The same, I guess."

"Great."

The girl left, and they were silent again for long while — watching the table or the far wall or the world outside.

"I don't usually drink in the afternoon," he offered once the waitress had brought their drinks and retreated behind the till. He looked around the room like a small boy caught smoking a cigarette or looking at magazines.

"Really? Sometimes that's the best time. Anyway, the season's old; it'll be dark in another half hour or so, if you have a sort of vampire thing about drinking red liquid when the sun is up."

"Well, no, I —"

"This wine could be my blood —" she intoned, not sure if she was quoting a book or a song. She held her glass with two fingers of her right hand, the fingers of her left running along the base of the stem. He watched the gesture and reddened slightly. "A toast?"

He laughed a sudden uncertain laugh. "Sure. What to? To us? To two strangers meeting? To possibilities?" He added in a low tone. His boldness rang false, somehow, ill fitting, like his one-size-fits-all shirt.

He brought his wine glass to his mouth, sampling the first taste, rolling it on his tongue. She spoke without raising her sight, watching instead the ruby liquid, and looking through it to the distorted image of the stained tablecloth behind.

"Or we could drink to truthfulness. Or to being ourselves."

"What —"

"Where do you think we'll go after this?"

"I, uh, I hadn't —"

"— thought it out? Back to your place, maybe?" Her tones were even and low, but with rising intensity. "Can we fuck at your place, or would it wake your wife or the kids? Or your mother? But maybe we'd be in the basement, so she wouldn't hear." She brought a finger to her lip and stroked it, as if feeling the shape of the words.

"I'm not —"

"— understanding? What? The rules? Basic human interaction?"

"Hey, you invited me over here."

"Did I? I must have missed that. What did I say? What did I offer? What sort of a deal have I made for services to be provided later, in exchange for — what —? What's the going rate for a smile?"

She looked up now, into his started gaze — poor child. She wanted to reach out — to pet his hand — but instead she raised her glass to eye level, then slowly began to pour it onto the table.

"Hey!" He scrambled up from his chair as a stream of wine pushed towards him. "What're you, nuts?"

"What's going on over there?" the waitress called.

"Nothing — I broke a glass." She replied, releasing her glass in response. It shattering in the middle of the pool on the table. Shards of glass and wine splattered her face and the front of her blouse, leaving her sparkling and bloodied.

"You're nuts!" he offered to the empty tables, to the grey man. "She's nuts!" he repeated to the waitress now at his side.

She looked up at the waitress — looked this young girl in the eyes — looked at her pale face and straight hair pulled back tightly, loose strands floating with the breath of the overhead fan. She watched the girl's pale lips part as she puzzled over what was to be said next — over how she was to establish her afternoon authority.

"He — said something," were the words she spread on the table for the pale girl to see. "He — suggested — wanted —"

"You'll have to pay for this," the pale girl said to the man. "I'll have to put this on your bill."

"Fine. Fine." He tossed a handful of bills and some change on the table. "Just so I can get the hell out of here."

He pulled his coat from the chair and rushed out into the dimming light. *To lick his wounds*, she thought. She heard the ring of the bell over the door, felt a brief push of cool night air.

"I'll — I'll get a cloth," the pale girl said before turning away and disappearing into the kitchen.

She reached forward, past the glass stem pointing like a compass needle to the empty chair, and dipped the tips of the fingers of her right hand into the wine and glass mixture in the middle of the table. She brought the red drops to her tongue, tasting the sudden bitterness, feeling the nick of something on the inside of her lip, feeling the sting of the wine finding her blood.

The Reluctant Poet

CANTO ONE

He had reached that point in his life when the need to sleep with other people easily exceeded the pleasure in doing so. The pursuit and desire seemed to reaffirm that he was still alive and attractive to others of his species, whereas the act itself had blended into the post-coital guilt of his ego's satisfaction. It had become a sort of messy paperwork to be dealt with before the next transaction. The obligation of product delivery after the ecstasy of closing the sale.

It bothered him, on occasion, that he had already begun to lose interest before the first garment hit the floor of her bedroom (or his own bedroom, or the room of a particular hotel he frequented on the fringes of downtown), his mind saying, 'Been there; done that,' when it should really have been asking the question, 'Can those be real?'

Was this normal? Was he normal?

But whom could he ask? To the few male friends whom he might describe as close, it could be interpreted as an admission that sex was not the pinnacle: the be-all and end-all of any relationship (unless they all believed as he did, but had never had the guts to talk about it — a level of conspiracy he could neither accept nor fathom).

Perhaps it was a male thing, a throwback to the hunter/gatherer/tribal mindset in which the kill was, ritualistically anyway, often more important than the feast. Or maybe it was a writer thing — he being a writer/publisher of a small regional magazine, *The Fishbinder* — the creative need to reinvent himself for his audience, to gain approval; the sharp contrast between the thrill of creation and the sexual equivalence of having to be in the room while they read it.

So, the question remained unasked and unanswered, and he continued through relationships where the duration of the pursuit routinely exceeded the time following the fall.

CANTO TWO

He'd first met Cindy — 'Cin' she liked to call herself — at a poetry reading at the local library. It was April, National Poetry Month (and all the false springs and grey, dashed hopes that represented), and he had been seconded by phone, based upon *The Fishbinder*'s status as one of the few surviving local publications and, therefore, cheap — the cultural equivalent of a downtown pimp — to supply several real live poets for the celebration — such as the celebration was: readings, cheese, wine, an audience of bored wannabes (failed poets themselves or else 'intellectuals' within the suburban limitations of the word), or people driven inside by the rain and wind to be captured by the lure of sweet black coffee and nameless snacks and the stain of cheap red wine.

"How delightful you were," she had told him. "So funny and real."

He was not supposed to have read that night. He had not, in fact, written a poem himself in many years (and even those tended to the coarse couplets usually seen scrawled in cubicles or glimpsed, in passing, spraypainted on bridge abutments). This despite the fact that his publication's audited books showed a monthly cheque to him as a "contributor" (although it could be argued that the cheque itself was a form of creativity). But that night one of his corral of poets had not shown up, and, rather than disappoint, he had decided, in the long silence after the name had been called and was beginning to thin on the air, that it was just easier to get up and read. He had a copy of the featured issue. No one knew who he was, thanks to his established practice of avoiding direct dealings with his writers — all of whom were of the anti-social variety usually categorized as 'pasty,' and, if truth be told, much preferred just to slip smudged envelopes under his office door at odd hours of the night, or submit by email, cloaking themselves in the anonymity of technology. And certainly no one knew the poet, except, perhaps, the closer members of his immediate family who had not yet been institutionalized.

So, he had stepped forward, assumed a slightly stooped posture at the podium, and began.

But partway in, no more than half a line, really, he was overcome by the fact that the piece he was reading was pure shit. And in an instant, in one of those public epiphanies one reads of in the lives of some of the lesser saints, he knew that it was all shit: every pretentious, meaning-laden, angst-dripping line of every ashen-faced prepositionally challenged poet he had printed in the last stanza of years. Either he had learned to dull his mind to it in an effort to cajole the work out of his writers so he could force out four issues a year only slightly behind deadline but within the terms of his federal arts grants, or the act of saying the words aloud had finally torn down a screen, and he now was able to see it for all it was. Shit. And not even the large solid kind that brings a sigh and a Hail Mary and a momentary glimpse into the workings of God's mind, but a stream of foul, putrid crap that couldn't even make a decent lump. Free verse diarrhea. Po-Mo ass gravy.

And he paused for a critical moment, as if for poetic emphasis. He briefly scanned the blank faces of his blank audience and made a fateful decision. He decided he would underline the pretension and the angst and the shittiness of the poem with an affectatious accent and a full-blown style and a pomposity that would have put even the most bilious of Victorian Shakespearean actors to shame. Shame! Shame!!

And they laughed. With him, for a change. So he upped the level of pomposity — just a touch — pushing it over the top inch by inch, until the 'top' became a mere speck far below. And they loved it. They devoured this opportunity to glance askance at the several readers who had come before him, each as serious as death (and as well received, if you assume that even Death would be greeted with a staccato of polite applause).

"You really are quite funny, Mr. Murdoch," she had continued, taking him by the hand and leading him to the small table to the side that served as a refreshment buffet. She reached into a box behind the bunting and took out a bottle of pinot noir. "Not for the general riffraff," she advised in a definitive whisper and poured them each a healthy draught into clear plastic glasses. "Cheers, Mr. Murdoch."

He started to speak — to correct her error — that not only was he not Mr. Murdoch, but neither was he funny or real or, most likely, anything else she might be thinking of him at that moment. But he met her eyes as she sipped her wine, and he returned her nod and dutifully partook of the pleasant offering, feeling a sort of transubstantiation.

"My name is Cindy Wellgrove. 'Cin,' to my friends."

"And retribution to your enemies," he replied, as a mock toast, the first words he had spoken since leaving the stage.

"You *must* join us after," she offered with a small laugh, leaning in close to him. "A few of the chosen — organizers and our inviteds — are going to finish off the donated wine just as soon as this is all over and we've shooed the rabble. Come, sit beside me. The next reader's coming on."

He did as he was told and took the hard-backed chair next to her.

For the next three poets, and the several days this seemed to entail, he feigned interest in the readers, all of whom he had published on occasion in *The Fishbinder*, none of whom, he now knew, he could be bothered to give the time of day to (or piss on if they were on fire, as his father had been wont to say). From time to time he would sneak glances to his right to assess this unknown Cin who seemed to admire him as someone else.

She wasn't beautiful, not in the classical sense, or even in the sense of the glossy magazines that sometimes filled his afternoons (or at least the twenty minutes right after lunch). But in her bright green eyes there was an energy, an intense immediacy for the task at hand he found tremendously appealing. Her hair was long, tied back, but with enough errant strands to suggest to him a kind of tousled sensuality that blended with the wine and piqued his interest. Her smile was pleasant, though her teeth were crowded into her mouth like dresses on a sales rack, and her lips were thin to the point of being nothing more than a line beneath a nose that flared too dramatically at its conclusion (not unlike most of the poems, he mused).

But she is so young, he thought, brushing a hand through his own greying and haphazard locks and counting his forty-five years to her — what? Thirty? Thirty-five? No more, he was certain. True, he had sported women younger in recent times, and had often regretted it the morning after the morning after, through a litany of pulled muscles and sprained appendages, but their energy had been only a physical energy, and here he thought he sensed an emotional and mental energy he had not faced in this millennium.

The poets continued, including a sound poet who seemed to be suggesting that the core meaning of life could be interpreted in a vowelsome resonance reminiscent of a flatulent smoke alarm.

Finally, though, the last syllable fell, dull and leaden, to the institutional carpet, followed closely by the flutter of thin applause.

Cin stood and thanked one and all with a short and pleasant speech that touched on involvement and beauty and support of the arts, but with a firm undertone that left no doubt that in ten minutes the doors would be locked and the hounds released to feast upon the tardy, so have a pleasant ride home.

"They're a harmless enough crowd," she confided to him on her return, "but I wouldn't say no to a canister of pepper spray and a freshly charged taser. Can I pour you another?"

And she did, without waiting for a nod or a wink. Clearly she is not used to rejection, he surmised, sipping again "the good stuff" as the last few poets were herded out and the auditorium doors pulled shut.

Now their group was down to a handful: one other organizer and a library assistant — men both, both younger than he, although one, he noted, had a good hundred pounds on him and could likely be scratched as a contender. The other — a husband? — (she was wearing a ring) — was too young and too fit to be trusted.

"Can I top that up for you?" she offered.

"Yes, thanks," he replied, unaware that he had been drinking. She emptied the bottle and moved to the table for reinforcements.

"Well, Mr. Murdoch, that was a spirited reading you gave," offered the thin one, while the heavy one drifted to the refreshment table to glean the remnants of the crackers and cheese tray.

"Thank you, but —"

"If that's your real name."

"Ah. I guess that now you've —"

"I've found that the best satirists often operate under a *nom de plume* — a sort of barricade from behind which they lob their *bon mots*."

"You got me," he replied to the self-satisfied grin the thin man wore like an out-of-date shirt. "The real name's Pinkney. Hamish Pinkney."

"Oh, really! Pull the other one: it has bells on it. No one's named Hamish Pinkney. If you must try a double-blind on me, at least pick a credible subterfuge. My name's Thomas — my real name," he winked. "That's Roger over there" — a distant hand waved, and crackers flew like startled pigeons. "And I think you're acquainted with Cin."

"Only in a theological sense."

"What? Oh, yes. Cin. Sin. Droll. Very earthy." And here he threw his head back and laughed a single bark, like the backfiring of a badly tuned car. "And what did you think of our cadre of artistes?"

"He suddenly wondered how many starving poets sit in Starbucks and drink ten-dollar coffees as they write their poems of poverty," she answered as she moved to them on cat's feet. A hollow metal clang grabbed at their attention.

"Jeez it, the fuzz!" Cin whispered with mock ferocity, leaning in and nodding her head towards the door. There stood a commissionaire of indeterminable age and gender who seemed to have been hired primarily for a markedly low centre of gravity.

"Ah, the gendarme. It must be the stroke of ten." Thomas tapped his watch for emphasis. "Perhaps we should repair to our usual après-event bistro."

With nods of agreement all around, and under the watchful eye of the ample security, they quickly packed away the remnants of the event into cardboard boxes of various sizes, stacked them behind the arras, and made their way on foot through the pale night the three or so blocks to a small wine-bar/coffee shop called Qasim's. There, amid the old wood and the white-washed walls and the stale hookah smoke and the framed pictures of exotic regions, they sipped their beer and wine and pale liqueur.

And before long he had gleaned the following very useful information: Roger was the chapter president of a local writers' group (failures all, but always there to administer an artistic 'group hug' to a damaged ego). Thomas was a self-proclaimed philosopher who liked to slum on occasion with poets and novelists, to allow them to bask in his intellectual superiority (to touch his mental arraignment, so to speak). During the day he stacked books in the library, hung about a downtown coffee shop, and dreamed great dreams for which the world was not yet ready. And he was not a rival.

From her he gathered more than he asked. Leaning in close, so close that he breathed in her faint skin scent of vanilla and jasmine, he learned she was married to an insurance broker who knew everything of actuary tables and statistics but nothing of art. "Counting everything but my value" she half-smiled, and he found a slim excuse to brush her hand with his fingertips while reaching for his drink.

But also he found that he would forever be Mr. Murdoch.

"Well, Mr. Murdoch, I was quite pleasantly surprised with your work," she said.

"Thank you, but I think you should —"

"I was beginning to despair that you would be like the rest: self-important, morose, and plump, with an adolescent viewpoint nurtured well into their forties."

"But there were moments," Thomas interjected. "The sound poet, as an exquisite example."

"Oh please," she cried, tossing her drink coaster at him, but catching Roger instead, knocking the handful of pretzels from his fist. "That pretty boy was so full of himself it was obscene to watch."

"At least he was trying — pushing to the edges — challenging what we find comfortable," Thomas pressed.

"You're a shameless modernist."

"Visionary, I prefer."

"He wasn't just no good himself, he made everything else in life seem duller and more commonplace and trivial. At least real poetry — even the classics — if they're bad, they just send you to sleep. But his stuff —"

"MacBeth doth murder sleep," Hamish offered in support.

"Exactly," she continued. "He makes you want to corner him with a pointed stick and ask him what the hell he was thinking, or find out where he lives, go there in the wee small hours, and kick him in the balls. I mean, he took up my limited time on this earth pretending to be a poet, which, where I come from, is still something to be."

"But what about the new," Thomas whined in imitation of argument. "What about the innovative? How are we to progress as artists if we mock the revolutionary? Would you have mocked Picasso, too, in his day?"

"Yes, Picasso was new and different. But to say someone's art deserves respect because it's new and different is beyond pretension. It's based on the assumption that everyone who runs a red light is an ambulance speeding to save human life. Well, thanks to him, this human life is now beyond saving."

"You exaggerate, my sweet one — you don the hairshirt of hyperbole to make your paper-thin point."

"Bullshit. And you wish I were your 'sweet one,' Thomas. Wade in here, Mr. Murdoch."

"Well, uh — I suppose —" he stammered.

"You have to do better than that, Mr. Murdoch. My honour is at stake here," and she tossed him a coy wink like small change.

"Well — I think that the only thing that makes art from a pile of garbage is coercion."

"Exactly! The slowly advancing pressure of the self-defined superior minds in their ivory towers."

"I think that there is such a thing as art," he continued, buoyed, "grounded in a universal language derived from all human experience and the absolutes of nature, and when you destroy the limitations and definitions of art by inclusion —"

"— via sterile decree —"

"— of absolutely everything, you destroy — well — everything."

"In supporting the destructive currents of modernism you are destroying the world. Well said, Mr. Murdoch. Game, set, match, Thomas. I tell you, if it weren't for the Canada Council grant, I'd chuck the whole thing and go back to doing the library's Saturday-morning children's book hour. Anyway," she continued, turning to Murdoch in a way that told Thomas he must seek other amusement, "Mr. Pinkney hadn't warned me that his group of poets would be largely a bunch of — do you like Mr. Pinkney?"

"I —"

"He struck me as either pompous or vague to the point of needing medical intervention when I spoke to him on the phone. Not all there," she added, tapping her forehead knowingly, shifting her chair closer to him.

"I've known him all my life."

"Oh."

"But I doubt if I'll ever figure him out."

"Ah. So —"

"Hmmm? Oh. Uh, Phillip."

"Phillip — Phil? Well, Mr. Phil Murdoch, I'm not familiar with your work, Phil. Where are you published?"

"Oh. Here and there."

"Surely *The Fishbinder* isn't your only outlet. That rag's not worth the recycled woodchip it's misprinted on."

"No! No. I — I have other — outlets."

"Being vague again, is he?" Thomas bellowed like a medieval innkeeper over his now spirited conversation with Roger on whatever Thomas felt was an appropriate topic he could dominate. Spirited in that Thomas was loud and animated whereas Roger sat like he'd been struck dead by a blunt instrument.

Thomas turned back to them. "I have my little theory about our good Mr. Murdoch. Anyone who can glean so accurately the foibles of the faint of rhyme must know a little something or two about how to do it properly. I think our Mr. Murdoch is a true poet. I think he was just pulling our literary legs. I think he has a few tricks up his sleeve. Some real meaty stuff under his hat."

"And nothing in his boots, Thomas? Somehow I think you're right. I'd like to read your real poetry sometime, Mr. Murdoch. There's nothing I like better than to curl up in bed with a good poem."

"Or a good poet," Thomas added with something of a wink that briefly chilled Hamish's blood, which was then immediately reheated by the sleepy look Cin draped his way.

Last call came much too soon, and they filtered back out into the night air. Pleasantries were exchanged, with a frivolous edge to mask any hint of real feelings. Although he wanted to pursue her further, no opening was offered, and he, tired from the weight of his new identity, finally decided to call it a night.

"Goodnight, Mr. Murdoch. It was a pleasure. You'll be top of my list if I ever organize another of these events —"

"I look forward —"

"— like that's going to happen while God's in Her heaven."

And she shook his hand and walked off to her car. He watched her drive away, sending a small wave after her into the darkness, before he opened his hand and looked at the crumpled paper she had slipped to him. No words, just ten numbers.

"Good morning," she whispered into his ear, gently drawing him forward from his dream to the half-light scene of rumpled sheets and discarded clothing.

"Good morning," he replied thickly, pulling into the warmth offered.

The path from there to here had been uncluttered.

"Hi," he had replied instinctively when she had answered the phone in that not-too-distant past.

"Hi."

"It's me — Murdoch — from the other night."

"Yes. I remember."

"You — I have a slip of paper you —"

"Lost?"

"Yes, I guess — well, I —"

"— thought you'd like to return it to me. How nice. Yes, I was wondering where I'd left my portfolio. How about —" here muffled voices, her hand clearly over the receiver "— coffee? Tonight? Say eight?" Each question sounded oddly like a statement to him. "No, no," she continued, as if he had spoken, "it's no imposition at all. I should be thanking you. Why don't we meet at that little café by the university —"

"Oscar's?"

"That's it. Yes, well — see you then."

Now it was several meetings later. Several chats in several different coffee shops, the discussion of poetry and writing having been gradually overtaken by more raucous laughter, more pointed innuendo, touches, first furtive then knowing and mutual, the kind of flirting he had not enjoyed since he was much younger. Then one night a casual "my husband's away for the evening" that caused his heart to flutter for a moment and his thoughts to stray.

"Coffee?" she offered now, and she slipped from the bed before he could reply. He watched her move to the coffeemaker in a slow rhythmic way that spoke volumes and reminded him why his testicles hurt. His penis, quiet 'til now, also stood up to get a better view. He hushed it with the spare pillow.

"Nothing special here, just your standard Columbian blend. Okay with you?"

"Sure."

She had already split open the pre-measured package and placed the filter in the standard-issue hotel machine.

"Oh, and it's just the powdered creamer," she reported as she spilled water from the carafe into the machine.

"I take it black."

"Good. Straightforward. Uncluttered. Me, too."

Buttons were pressed and the machine began to gurgle. She turned her eyes back to him; he turned his to the pillow.

"I think we should talk," she began.

"Sure, if you —"

"I'll start. This is a regular sort of thing for you, isn't it?"

"What —"

"This."

"Well, I wouldn't —"

"The desk clerk knew you. You got your 'regular' room. The next stay is free."

"Sometimes, perhaps. It's such a bore having to keep my apartment clean just in case. And, well, it keeps it all to a more manageable —"

"Level of commitment?"

"Yes. If you like. Are you going to finish all of my sentences?"

"I've yet to meet a writer who couldn't use a good editor."

"Quite." He put the pillow aside, no longer needing it.

"This is a first for me."

"Oh."

"Well, a first this calendar year, give or take. And if we're to continue I'm going to expect a little production from you."

"Oh."

"I'm attracted to you because you're a poet. But from what I can see, your production is pretty much limited to a few poems published in backwater rags and some scribbles you keep telling me aren't yet ready to be seen."

"Yes, you see —"

"That's just not going to cut it, my man."

"Really, it's a matter of —"

"You're going to have to do better."

"Ah."

"But enough on that. Coffee's ready." And with that she snapped the conversation shut and poured them each a coffee, black.

Now he knew the ground rules: creative production would equal sexual gratification. Normally he would never have succumbed to such a blatant carrot/stick, but later, when she had left to return to her own world (even with a husband out of town, she would never stay into the languid portions of the morning) and he was alone in the room, he tried to think it out, to rationalize his compulsion (or was it an impulsion — an interior drive rather than an exterior).

He was not truly a sexual hunter, although he sometimes would joke to himself that over his two-score and five he'd had more woman than Colonel Sanders had had chickens (meaning no disrespect to the Colonel). But she was different. In her sexual aggression and low cries of pleasure was a passion he had lost in himself — a passion whose edges he was able, at times, to draw around himself, to hide away within. And suddenly his life started to make sense. Now he found he had focus. True, it was all sexual, but a focus is a focus.

As well, from this passion, he found over the next several months that he had become a writer. His old sense of ennui and overpowering feeling of inevitable failure were now replaced with something like joy at picking up a pen. And joy was also something he'd assumed had long ago packed its bags and left with no forwarding address.

True, his initial writing efforts were fragmented, but he found, when he had pushed a bundle of crumpled scraps across the table to her, she would occasionally pause to reread something and sigh a single word.

"Yes".

"It's good?"

"Oh no. Not in itself. But it speaks to me of potential — that maybe you're hiding something more from me. What are you hiding from me?" And she would sweep the papers from the table as she reached for his hand, the scraps scrambling to the floor like startled birds seeking a new roost. And as she would kiss him, pushing her tongue into his mouth, a single thought would tear through the curtain of his arousal.

"Oh God, what am I going to write next time?" What offering would be enough to meet her insatiable expectations? He knew the joy was temporary. He had read too much Darwin to trust in the lasting presence of joy.

CANTO FOUR

"Morning, Mr. Pinkney."

"Morning, Enid."

"Nice to see you again."

"Nice to be seen."

It had been a little over two weeks since he had last been in his office at *The Fishbinder*. In fact, over the five or so months since he had first encountered 'Cin,' his appearances had been something less than frequent ("sightings" was how Enid referred to them). Enid, a girl of nineteen or so, with so many rings pierced through one eyebrow that it looked like someone had stolen her shower curtain, handed him a stack of pink phone message slips. He fanned them like a losing hand of gin.

"This is it?"

"Forty-seven. Not enough?"

"I mean it's nothing but —"

"Writers? I think the fact that the next issue is already four weeks late is starting to concern them."

"They should be happy anyone would even consider reading their shitty little babblings in the first place. If they expect to make a living as poets, they should get used to hanging out at the bus station, panhandling for half-smoked cigarettes and small change. Any mail?"

"I've given all the bills to Shirley to do up the cheques. Whether or not you sign them will be between her and yourself, I'm guessing."

"Her and you."

"What?"

"The reflexive pronoun doesn't apply," he heard his editor's voice say, intended as a sort of covering smoke for his retreat into his office. But Enid was too quick.

"There's a letter from the Arts Council advising that you're not meeting the terms of your grant and threatening a repayment order," she fired back. "Oh, and this." She handed him a plain brown envelope, oversized, with a typed address label and no return. "It's addressed to Mr. Murdoch, but at this address, so I'm guessing you can open it."

"Thanks."

He turned to his office.

"Mr. Pinkney?"

"Yes."

"Am I still going to have a job here in, say, the next few months."

"As long as the magazine exists, you'll have a job."

"That's what I was afraid of. What's happened, Mr. Pinkney?"

"What's happened?"

"You used to care about the magazine. You used to care about poetry. You used to show up."

"I've changed, Enid. I've begun to know things. I used to be a romantic in that I used to think you had to be a decent person to write well. I now know that's not true. I once thought it a thrill to sit at home at night, a glass of wine in hand, reading poetic manuscripts. But in reality, it's painful. And always has been. Which is why I began to only do it early in the morning, so it wouldn't be my last task before I drifted to sleep, the tepid verse seeping into my dreams. Or leave it until I was hungover or constipated, and life held little hope anyway. Or, best of all, not to do it at all. Now I keep the glass of evening wine and omit the manuscript altogether."

"Thank you, Mr. Pinkey," Enid replied, after a long blink.

He opened the glass door of his office, noting that the top of the *P* in *Pinkney* was beginning to unstick from the glass, as if it were deflating.

His office was clutter. Bookshelves lined two walls, from floor to ceiling, holding books that stood at all possible angles of equilibrium. More books were stacked on the floor, like African anthills or a literary Stonehenge, as if the light through the wood slat blinds would eventually align with the volumes to reveal a fundamental truth or at least the correct time.

He closed the door and took the swivel chair behind the wooden desk and dropped the pink phone messages next to the previous piles, like droppings from a poorly trained flamingo. But the envelope he held for several moments, staring at the address label, recognizing the slightly misaligned *M* that was characteristic of the aging Underwood on the side table.

He turned the envelope over in his hands, his fingers moving slowly to the sealed flap. He took a deep breath, like a diver standing over a cold plunge. Then his senses were full with the hasty tear of paper.

Where he expected to find, as had been the case over the last few months, several sheets of typed paper with a stub of mimeographed sheet clipped to the upper corner, this time there was only a single sheet. Letterhead. His poems had been kept. Where he expected to hear the Hallelujah Chorus, there was instead the buzz of the intercom.

"Mr. Pinkney, I've got Phillip Murdoch on line one."

"Tell him to fuck off."

"I told him that last time."

"Then he should be used to it."

"Righteo."

The type was simple; the message spoke volumes. By the third reading, he scanned past the "Dear Mr. Murdoch" and settled quickly onto paragraph three — past the salutations and rationalizations, to the part that, despite each successful reading, continued to say "we are most interested in publishing, in our fall issue, three of the poems you submitted, and feel, with some not unaggressive input from our editors, that a more substantial publication could be . . . payment would be negotiated at our current rates . . . we look forward . . . Constance Blight, Acquisitions Editor."

And it never changed. With each reading it was the same.

He swivelled his chair to gaze out the window behind his desk (or at least that portion of the window not obscured by dirt or pieces of cardboard standing in for broken glass panes).

There was a certain irony (if that was the word — fifteen years in publishing, and he could never remember the difference between irony and coincidence): he was a publisher himself. He could easily have devoted an entire issue to his own work. But to have a handful of poems vetted by a professional — Constance Blight, no less — accepted by a publication that was actually read — a publication you could find at the corner newsstand or displayed prominently in one of the box-type bookstores so cursed by the literati and praised by the buying public — here was a true measure of success.

And success was what he coveted. He admitted that now, fanning the letter slowly and feeling the breeze, like a lover's touch, brush back his hair. He could feel a new self starting to tear at the stained cocoon he had wrapped himself in, in the name of — what? Respectability? Hardly. Stability? No. Fear? Yes, that was it. Fear. Fear of success.

He did the quick math in his head. Total payment would be in the range of forty-five dollars for the poems. Perhaps more if they decided to publish an entire — no. Relax. Don't get ahead of yourself, he thought. Forty-five dollars is good. A good start. He would squander it on champagne — domestic — or maybe a four-pack of one of those really good specialty beers.

"Mr. Pinkney."

He felt suddenly exhilarated. A din bird stooped dully on the broken drain line of the chemical works opposite seemed to him like a dove, the broken shard of nesting in its beak like a branch of greenery telling of life and paradise at hand.

"Mr. Pinkney!"

"Hmmmmm?"

Enid stood in the doorway, black-painted nails tapping at the glass of the partially open door.

"There's a lady here to see you."

"Tell her I'm out."

"She knows you're in. We could hear you humming from the reception area."

"What does she want?"

"I don't know. She wouldn't say. Her name is Cindy Welgrove."

"The asshole ducked me."

"Really?"

"He was in there. Any fool could tell. I could see his shadow on the glass of his office door. He was humming *Jesu, Joy of Man's Desiring* loud enough to rattle windows."

"A much-misunderstood hymn, if you ask me."

"The prick was through the window and down the fire escape before you could say *La Belle Dame San Merci*."

"The bastard. Uh, what — if you don't mind me asking — um — what — what were you — I mean, if it's not too impertinent of me — what —"

"— did I want to talk to the little bastard about? About you, naturally."

"Naturally."

"I wanted to talk to him about you — to get some back issues of the magazine to see your work — anything of yours he may have published. But more, I wanted to get him to release you from this unholy hold he seems to have on you."

"Hold —?"

"You've been writing for how long, and he's the only magazine who'll have you? I can't believe that. For some reason you feel compelled to submit only to him."

"Impelled."

"What?"

He placed his glass of wine on the bedside table.

"An internal force, not an external."

He used her silence to listen to his heart pack its bags and catch the next bus to his throat.

"Explain yourself, then. Why him? Why that rag?"

"I — I — I like it?"

"Like it?"

"I'm sentimental. They were there when I was just starting out. They published my first work. They believed in me — Pinkney believed in me."

She seemed to believe him, and he dug himself deep into the layers of sheets and blankets still warm from their nocturnal actions. She stood by the small alcove where the sink and coffee maker were and refilled her own glass with cabernet from the nearly spent bottle.

"You deserve better," she continued.

"Do I?" came his muffled voice.

"Of course you do. Your past self — what you read at that first gathering and the little you gave me initially — I mean it was all very nice and safe and whimsical and everything, but what you've been creating recently — well, it simply blows your old shit right out of the water."

"Is that really what one wants to do with shit? Blow it out of the water? I mean, isn't it better left in the water? Isn't the past best flushed away without regret?"

"Oh, do shut up."

"Of course."

"Don't give me that damned whipped puppy look. If we're going to get your writing up and out of the mire, you've got to sever your old ties — dump Pinkney and his fuckrag of a *Fishbinder* like yesterday's dregs."

"And what if —"

"What?"

"If — well — if some of that old — some of my stuff was already —"

"What are you saying?"

"Nothing."

"What if some of your new work was already published in one of the swankier magazines?"

"Sure. What . . . if?"

"I'd know. I'd have to know. You'd have shown them to me in order to brag or to win my favours. If some new work exists and I don't know about it, it would mean you've been going behind my back. And I couldn't tolerate that kind of deception."

"You'd consider it —"

"Disloyalty. Betrayal. Unfaithfulness. But why discuss this? It's not true, is it?"

"Of course not — I was just —"

"Jeez, now you've got my blood up. Was that your plan, you sex monkey? Bring me to the boil with your damned creative impudence?"

"What else?"

And she tossed her empty wine glass to the floor, dropped her robe and moved towards the bed in a manner that awoke in him a sexual panic measurable on the Richter scale.

CANTO SIX

The act of writing — the physical act of putting words on paper — was not foreign to him. He had spent years composing correspondence and grant proposals — both legitimate forms of fiction — rejecting writers and begging for cash.

He'd never had much money, and he had less now. And he was no fool (at least as far as finances went). He knew that a few poems published here or there every other month or so was not going to do it. He needed a book. But he had no financial cushion to get him through a concentrated time of writing, the time it would take to put a manuscript together. He needed either to expand his cash reserves or manipulate the fabric of time.

But to this end he suddenly found himself rich with a certain incentive. A recent poem of his, "Someone's in the Kitchen with Dianthus," had appeared in the literary journal *Anaphora* and had garnered some attention. This included an unexpected letter of offer in the afternoon post from the publishing house of Mensch, Mensch, and Fullfederhalter, who were offering a pretty penny (although not many of them) for a poetry manuscript to fill an opening in their fall lineup due to the sudden incarceration of one of their poets for crimes of a whisperable nature — but only if he could submit it within two weeks, double-spaced and without typographical errors (although their letter said *without typographical erros*, which he took to suggest merely their lack of editorial staff as opposed to some sort of misspelt literary primness).

From his time publishing *The Fishbinder*, he had always believed that there was a thin line between panic and creativity, but then he had been on the side of providing the panic, not the creativity. But this opportunity inspired him to visit his old office one last time, in the wee hours of a dark night, to pull up some loose floor boards, secure an aging tin cash box from its resting place, and use the few crumpled bills and tarnished coins to settle into a fourth-floor bachelor suite under his new name of Murdoch.

But how to start?

He remembered his writing ritual from his youthful days of composing poems to catch the attention of pale and dark-haired women. First he placed his writing desk — a swaybacked card table — beneath a window, to allow for an urban vista suitable for long, unfocused stares. Second, he laid out quality paper — A5 sized, wood/cotton blend, 120 gsm weight, with impeccable sheen and smoothness. Third, a fresh bottle of Pilot Iroshizuku Kon-Peki ink in a shade of midrange cerulean blue. He preferred using a fountain pen. Something with a substantial weight and a palladium nib. It was the pen his father had given him. In truth, it was all his father left him — left behind, really, when he and his mother had disappeared in a hurry together late that hot August night when he was seventeen, leaving him with $378 in cash against the rent of $485 owing on the one-bedroom apartment. It had been tough, yes, but he didn't hate them for it. Sometimes the parents feel a need to leave the nest first, before the first of the month, leaving no forwarding address. It nurtures in the offspring a sudden independence and resourcefulness, and an ability to quickly determine in the uncertain world who is your friend and who, quite decidedly, isn't.

And why he should remember this? Why should this late adolescent thought come unbidden to him just as he put pen to paper to begin his first poetry manuscript? Why should it come to prominence just as the first free-flow of ink moved across the page with a frictionless and unconscious ease? He had no idea. But he awoke three days later, slumped over this desk, a puddle of drool stringing from his lip to the wooden surface, and just over sixty pages scribed in a varied but legible hand.

With almost mechanical fluidity, he bound the papers together with a large metal clip, slipped them into an oversized envelope, then wrote the publisher's address on the label and his own address (with his recently assumed name) in the upper left. He slapped a palm full of stamps in the upper right, unaware of the total value but reasonably sure it was sufficient to send anything up to the weight of a moderate dog through the post. Then he left his apartment, shoeless and in his golf shirt and sweat pants, and walked to the mailbox on the corner.

Up to this moment, it had all been like a dream. But he felt, and he would always remember feeling, an odd emptiness — a sense of loss — when he finally put the envelope in the mail slot and heard the hollow thud of it landing.

Against all norms and rules of submission, he had not kept a copy of the manuscript 'for his files.' He trusted to the fates and the thin veneer of chivalry that can still be found in some corners of the writing word, that his work would be respected. *Quis erit, erit.* What will be will be.

He squinted up at the new morning sun, counted the last of the coins in his pocket, and slumped into a corner shop for a cup of sweet black coffee and a glazed cruller, finally feeling like a true writer.

CANTO SEVEN

Tuxedoes. Formal gowns. The air thick with salutations and the type of 'My God just talking to you has saved my soul from an eternity in purgatory' sort of greetings only experienced at award ceremonies.

Sixteen months have passed. The universe has edged several billion miles farther asunder in this blink of the cosmic eye, and all in its wake lies broken and bleeding.

He had simply stopped returning her calls. He liked to think of it more an issue of omission rather than any sort of act of moral consequence (and any discussion using the phrase 'passive/aggressive' would have been met with a silencing 'tut-tut' and a raised hand and an innocent widening of the eyes).

And she, finding herself in the unfamiliar role of the jilted lover (the monotone of his voicemail message coming closer, each time, to shattering her resolve into shards of invective and hard consonants). Because the first call is one of social intercourse — of human need. The second is almost one of courtesy or concern. But it is the third call — the third attempt to cross what is just then defining itself as a void — a relationship blackhole from which no emotion will ever escape again — it is then that one is put in the unenviable position of donning the mantle of fool. And once that threshold has been crossed, the options are simple: continue to call until the police finally come with a restraining order and pry the receiver from your white knuckles, using hardware normally reserved for vehicular mishaps; or fade quietly into the past.

As for him, he found it a very simple progression: lust waning first to desire, then desire to nostalgic lamentation, then, finally, to simple nostalgia — all in the name of survival.

He took another glass of champagne from the waiter's tray, but placed it down on a small side table so he could adjust his cummerbund and follow his suspenders with his hand to try and find the origin of the twist that had mysteriously materialized.

"Murdoch, my son my trout — I have found you and now you shall be mine."

His flinch was not due to being called 'Murdoch' in public (indeed, the legal name change would be official within the week), but rather from Thomas's mincing falsetto loud enough to cause his glass to vibrate within a breath of explosion.

"Thomas. What brings you here?"

"I am a patron of the arts at all levels. And this — a major publishing coronation unlike any other —" here he made a sweeping gesture that exposed the frayed cuff of his shirt and showed that his jacket was badly in need of repair "— draws me like Trilby to Svengali, like —"

"— a moth to a flame?"

"Hmmmm? Yes! I like that. Clearly you are a writer my dear Mr. Murdoch, but then I've always known that." He leaned in close and breathed surreptitious tones over the satin of Murdoch's lapels. "And I have read your thin volume, Mr. Murdoch, and I ached for your passion. I wept. I searched the wine cellar of my soul and found it wanting."

"One cabernet short of a vintage."

"Precisely, sir. Precisely. *Exactement.* Couldn't have said it better myself."

"Oh, I'm sure you could — given enough tries."

"High praise indeed. You're too kind. I do, of course, wish you the best. You are up against formidable opposition. Yvette St. Poisson's *Fish Paste Pottage* for example, and, of course, Igor Rocmisoksoff's *Curses My Mother Wept Upon the Summer Morn My*

Virgin Youth Was Misplaced Amongst the Desert Ferns is enough to make one —"

"I did. All over the chaise lounge."

"Then you know."

"But —" he turned to look directly at Thomas. "But — is it — is my book really . . . good?"

Thomas was caught — the sincerity of the question slipping through the layers.

"Yes."

"I wonder that all the time — that, and how I got here — to this pinnacle, low as it might be."

"How? You put in the work, my dear fellow. You did something that most writers fail to do — you stopped taking about writing and actually wrote."

"I suppose I did."

"Trust me: writers are never more creative than when they're coming up with reasons not to write. And, of course, you distanced yourself from *The Fishbinder* and sought out a real publisher."

"*The Fishbinder*," he repeated sadly.

"If you'd stayed there your writing would have gone down with that rag. As it is, it disappeared below the surface without a ripple. Lord know what became of the editor."

"Pickney."

"Yes. He disappeared like a cheap novel left behind on a bus, unregretted."

"All those writers left without an outlet."

"Oh, don't you worry a squib about them. Several have banded together to start their own collective complete with a monthly printing. *The Rhyme of the Month*, I think they're calling it."

"How unfortunate."

"Indeed. It does illustrate a certain virginal lack of awareness. But then, they are minor poets. No, my dear fellow, do not question yourself. You are here on this literary high ground for two reasons: your talent and destiny."

"Destiny? But whose? Divine destiny seems a little presumptuous."

"But the other —?"

"Too accurate. Too filled with the facts — too laden with the choices I've made."

"And those choices are rounding off the edges of your enjoyment? My dear Mr. Murdoch, art is a philosophy of despair — the legacy of an already discarded past. We must destroy in order to build — the stones of the last temple are the foundations of the new."

"Which themselves are destined to become the buried foundations of the next?"

"All fame is fleeting. Where society isn't bourgeois it strives to become so. Natural selection. Not to dominate for the moment you are given is to go against nature."

"Well, if anyone would know about going against nature, it's you, Thomas."

"That is unworthy of you, Mr. Murdoch, unless I choose to interpret it as high praise again. Which I shall. But if you're wondering how tonight will unfold, it won't be long before the literary Rubicon is crossed."

"What?"

"Before they announce the winner. Before all is known — oh! There's Ogden Pardue, the bitch. I must say 'Allo'."

And with that he directed theatrical kisses to Murdoch's cheeks and disappeared on a wave of lavender and crème de menthe liqueur. Murdoch retrieved his champagne glass and took a swallow that could be called generous by anyone's standards.

He moved slowly, without purpose, from his end of the large foyer closer to the exit and to the hotel bar. The podium and microphone were a few feet away, beneath a brightly lettered banner that announced this event as the 17th annual, bearing the logo of the sponsoring beer company more prominently than the event itself.

He had stopped near the door, idly brushing dust from the leaf of a large plastic fern with his event program, when he saw her. She was near the refreshment table, a speared cocktail weenie halfway to her open mouth, talking to a squat man in a tartan tuxedo. She was dressed in a simple black dress that said to him things that still could not be uttered on AM radio.

She looked up in an accidental manner, meeting his gaze with a casualness that compelled him to move towards her. With a polite nod and a whispered word to the tartaned gentleman, she moved a few paces in his direction, not halfway, but enough to illustrate a détente.

"You look wonderful."

"You as well," she smiled, perhaps remembering how uncomfortable he was with compliments. "It's your big night, possibly."

"Awards, they don't really mean anything."

"That's because you've never won one. They are intoxicating, leaving you in the thrill of the moment, unable to speak or think or remember those who lifted you out of the muck and mire."

"Ah."

"That was the champagne talking."

"Not as bubbly as I would have hoped."

"This isn't really how I envisioned our next encounter. I saw less glitz, more blood and frequent use of the word 'betrayal.'" She offered a small but not reassuring smile.

"I've hurt you, haven't I?"

"Oh, there's that insightful writer's edge. Wait — how did the *Advocate's* reviewer put it? *In tune with the romantic psyche.*"

"He was a bit overdone."

"No shit. Which is probably why he isn't working there anymore. 'Difference of artistic opinion,' he'd probably suggest, which would be right. He thought he was good. They didn't. The contrary opinion prevailed. More champagne?" She lifted two glasses from a passing tray, offering one across the space between them with something like a reluctance. His fingers glanced hers as he took the offering.

"But really," she continued, "the *Advocate's* nothing more than a local paper — a community paper, if you like — garden shows and yard sales. Cattle and chattel. Now the *Sentinel's* the paper you really need to catch the eye of."

"Yes. The *Sentinel's* a good paper. Very influential."

"Fuck influential. They're kingmakers in the writing business. A kind word can make a local writer's career. And when they dump on you, you stay dumped. Nothing will scrub the stink off you. They could send Atwood back to waiting tables."

He fidgeted with his glass, turning it in his hand, feeling the burrs of the cheap stemware.

"I suppose —"

"But is that fair? Is it fair that so much power is concentrated in so small an area? I mean awards are nice — even this beer mug and handful of loose change tonight — assuming you do win — but the Sentinel's review would really push your book onto the national stage, wouldn't it? Get you into the box stores. Maybe even an *O* on the cover."

"I suppose —"

"So they are really the difference between a local success and all the mall openings and speak-for-food Rotary lunches you can handle, and a national success and some level of financial recognition."

"Why are telling me —?"

"Oh, no reason. Conversation."

A tall man with a greying expression moved to the podium and began to shuffle papers. The crowd turned expectantly to him. Cin moved close to Murdoch but waved over to the tartaned gentlemen in a soft fashion. The tall man began to speak, but his words were lost as Cin leaned in close and whispered in his ear.

"It hurt me like hell when you dumped me, I'm not too proud to say. It caused a lot of soul searching, but in many ways that can be good, can't it. Reevaluation of priorities. Reassessment of goals and objectives. I ended my marriage, for example. No great loss, really, unless you consider his undeclared investment accounts. But renewing for me, in a sense. And financially advantageous. And I've sought out new relationships. Better relationships. Influential relationships."

He blinked and turned his gaze from the podium, but could not face her.

"Such as my current relationship," she continued. "There he is: the one in the tartan tuxedo. Oh, I never introduced you. What a silly oversight on my part. Brador Woo is his name. He's the new literary critic at the *Sentinel*."

And he closed his eyes, crushed his program in his hand, and lost entirely the words of the tall man at the podium.

". . . and the winner is —"

STICK PEOPLE

The house needed repainting. She could see that now, as she stood in the driveway looking up. Not the whole house. The siding was fine — dirty, but nothing a power washer wouldn't clean up — but the paint around the windows was chipped and peeling. Maybe the whole window needed replacing. She couldn't remember how old they were. Maybe they were original to the house, and that would make them twenty? Twenty-five? And there had been frost in the corners of the glass all winter, and that's a sign of leakage, isn't it? Warm air escaping? Cold getting in? Thermodynamics, it was called. At least it was called that on the high school test that she thought she'd aced but only got a B+ on. And that was a long time ago. Almost as long as the house. Longer than her marriage.

The weather was warmer now. The snow was gone, except for insistent ridges lurking in the shadows. Spring was a promise on the verge of being fulfilled. At least that was what the poets would say. Although she hadn't read a poet since college. After she quit partway through. "One trimester into my second term," she'd sometimes joke to herself, practising her ironic look in the bathroom mirror. That bathroom mirror had seen a lot of looks.

Stacy and Bradley were with their father for the weekend. It was time for chores. Spring cleaning. That's what good neighbours did in the spring. Raked away the dead grass. Picked up the debris of winter. That's what Frank used to do. Chores. Wash the van in the driveway. Wave at the neighbours. Call out names. And that's what she would do. Except she couldn't remember their names. And they were nowhere to be seen.

And she'd cheated. She'd used the automatic wash at the gas station on the corner, the one next to the strip mall. Paid the extra $8.95 after the gas fill for the ultra-wash. Or was it the Supreme? Or the Deluxe? There'd been three choices, she remembered, all of them superlatives. And she'd paid the most for the best. It was the kind of car wash where you drove into a building. Stayed in your car while machines did all the work.

She'd felt oddly exhilarated enclosed in the van in the small block building, buffeted by the blasts of water until she was vibrating with the van, pink foam obscuring her view of the world then revealing it again with a flush of fresh water, everything clearer than before. And she'd driven out slowly, through the roar of the overhead dryer, watched the water drops defy gravity and climb the windshield onto the roof. Evaporate. Disappear as if by magic. As if by intention. As if they'd been planning it for a while.

As she'd waited to turn onto the main street, waited in the approach next to the brick and stone entrance sign that delineated this neighbourhood of superlatives, whose name commemorated the oaks that had perished in its construction or had never existed, she felt a brief moment of being clean and pure and new. But that clicked away with the roll of the odometer as she drove back, picking up that layer of dust again as she passed the trim hedges and trim houses full of trim people — down the curving streets — not a straight road in sight, no way to get a clear view of where you're going. On her cul-de-sac she waved at what she thought were faces in the windows watching her return, at shadows she saw flitting behind the glass and curtains.

Back home, the van parked in the driveway, fingerprints of winter grime still visible on the bottom of the rear bumper, like a monster under the bed, she realized something wasn't right. So she went into the garage. Found a putty knife among the tools hanging up above the work bench. Removed it from the hook, leaving its painted shadow on the backboard — a symbol of Frank's need for order. A place for everything. Ready evidence of order betrayed. She took the putty knife and moved to the back of the van.

The window shone almost black in the mid-afternoon sun, like a void. The figures were white, stark — stick figures representing a perfect family, but without flesh or depth, defined by their activities.

She remembered when they'd bought the van, traded in the rusted sports car for it. The car she'd bought for college. The one she'd paid for with her own money after working three shit jobs, so she could move out west. Escape her parents, using the unimpeachable logic of further education. She remembered how Frank saw these figures at the dealership, wanted to add them, as if he were hanging her and the kids on the back window like his tools in the garage.

"It's fun," he'd said and smiled that humourless smile of his, and she'd said yes because she didn't want to be unfun. Not in front of the salesman. Not in front of the kids.

She remembered how she was forced to choose — to pick out a predetermined activity — to define herself by someone else's narrow choices.

Frank, of course, had his hockey — the tall figure holding a hockey stick like a shepherd's crook. Soccer was easy. Bradley was into soccer. And Stacy fell in love with the little stick girl in the tutu, despite there being a soccer girl as well.

"But you play soccer, too," she'd said, trying to guide Stacy, hearing thin echoes of her mother's voice.

"But so does Bradley. But he doesn't dance, and I do." Stacey had surprised her with her defiance. Was it supposed to begin so soon? So desperate to define herself, her role on the back of the van, by what made her distinct from her older brother.

And Ranger. There was even a small dog figure that looked oddly like Ranger, assuming Ranger could ever sit still long enough to be drawn, even as a stick figure. Small. White. Head tilted. Tongue hanging moist from a mouth dripping enthusiasm.

But when it came to something that defined her there was nothing. No stick figure of frustration. No stick figure of unfulfilment. Nothing that showed loneliness in the midst of others, or the kind of aching sense of loss and terror that wakes a stick figure up in the middle of the night to spend hours listening to the sounds of the neighbourhood solidifying around her. Just soccer and dance and tennis and yoga. And shopping.

So she chose shopping. A stick woman with arms wide, a shopping bag in each hand, hair dishevelled in a way that was supposed to make her look frazzled, but was more like an explosion of electrical wires. A hard day at the mall. This wasn't her either. She had a job, or at least a place to go during the day once the kids were at school — assuming they weren't sick, or the teachers didn't have a PD day, or she could be bothered to get up. But the figure was less not her than any of the others, and that made sense at the time. And she liked the hair.

But now she knew the figures had to go. God only knew if they had ever represented their family, but now, well. Bradley didn't play soccer anymore. Video games, mostly. And cigarettes with his friends, she suspected. Stacy's sense of self was more bookish, and she'd grown so much, so awkwardly, so unlike a dancer. And Frank. Well, that was obvious. Unless she was going to add Monica to the van. Monica who was already a stick figure. Did they have stick figures for what Monica and Frank did, she wondered? Did they have stick figures for betrayal?

Even Ranger. He'd run off, too, some years ago. Or was carried off by coyotes — the ones she'd hear at night in the distance, circling the limits of the subdivision. The ones he used to bark at so furiously in his defence of the backyard. Perhaps if she'd barked a little more. At Frank. At Monica. Herded the kids more closely.

Ranger. Who named a small, white lap dog Ranger? Ranger was a name for a noble dog. One that hunted. That blazed a trail. That saved little Timmy from the well. That stood firm and fought off an army of coyotes. But Frank had had a golden retriever named Ranger when he was young. And she had insisted that it be a small dog because of the kids. And because she had no experience with dogs. To make it easier. Plenty of room left when everyone was gone and the dog named Ranger shared her bed on a workday, well into the slanting light of late morning.

She pressed the edge of the knife against the glass, but was suddenly worried. What if she scratched the window? Can you scratch a car window with metal? She couldn't remember. She couldn't remember a single high school test that covered this. Diamond would scratch it, sure. Diamond cut everything. But metal? With her luck, yes. With her luck the glass would shatter into those thousand little beads at her first touch — the sudden way safety glass explodes. Just what she needed: another bill. Another expense. Another invoice to place on the kitchen counter near the phone. To stick to the fridge door with magnets, to be handy when the collection call came. Another reason to just run screaming from this whole shit world she seemed to find herself in now. Not that she'd be missed. The kids would fend for themselves. They'd survive. They were young. They'd glean. They'd grow a new tail. Like lizards. She remembered that from a distant test.

She pressed her head again the glass and felt the coolness, the resistance, the surety that it would not shatter, or give way suddenly to swallow her into the blackness. But it was a lie, too. And she found herself first falling — her thoughts spinning and tumbling like lost socks in the dryer — then she was running in a field, a herd of coyotes and white dogs rolling and howling around her feet. The sun at her back. The wind like a hand on her face, fingers in her hair. Giving chase to something far in the distance where the woods began.

But a distant car horn stopped the dogs in their tracks and tugged at her flying hair, and she pulled back with a start, unsure how much time had passed. She caught her reflection still trapped in the depths of the glass, so much like she used to be but so different. The eyes more tired. Circles around them like rings from coffee cups. The unfocused look. Everything seemed familiar, but sagging with the edges rubbed indistinct. Like a school friend at a reunion.

The knife was still in her hand, still against the glass, just beside a white head. She finessed the knife edge under a border and felt surprise at how easily the figure came away — how the white circle cast a sudden reflection in the glass and seemed to grow a third dimension.

She pushed further, slowly, enjoying the feeling of power. Soon the tall hockey player was curling down, first with a nod of his head, then a deep samurai bow, finally a prostrate supplication, deflated. In a slow handful of seconds he was floating to the pavement as if freed from all substance, the gentlest of fluttering suicidal leaps to the pavement.

Ranger was next. But him she caught. Laid him out in her open hand, as if for the first time in his short life he were obeying a command to lie down. To stay. Ranger she'd save. Put him on the fridge, maybe, to guard the bills and notices. Or maybe she'd find his metal bowl in the box in the basement and mark his ownership on the side. To say he'd once been there — that he'd existed. In another time. Like a cave painting.

She had planned to remove them all, but now she liked the look of the three of them remaining, the way she watched over the dependent two with open arms. She removed the soccer ball at Bradley's feet with a sweep. Trimmed Stacey's frilly tutu until it looked more like a dress. But something else was wrong.

She put the knife again against the glass, this time pressing the edge to make a small cut and then another. Then she carefully peeled away the shopping bags until they fell from tired hands to the pavement.

Now the woman on the glass took on a different look. Defiant. Don't fuck with me. She towered over the children like a god. Her hair was still in full disarray. Her arms were still out from her sides, but now the hands that had carried the weight of the bags were fists.

DOWNSIZING

"Before you start, would you like some tea?"

It's a ritual, I think, with the women of a certain age, the grandmothers — especially if there's English or Scottish blood in them. Tea is a way of greeting — the social equivalent of two dogs sniffing. It's a chance to organize, to introduce, to enquire, to prepare for the task at hand.

"Thank you, Mrs. Griffin, that would be nice."

My task was simple: I had to pack up and move items from a house to a small apartment in an old block downtown. She was lucky. She'd be in her own place, not a condo in one of those medi-centres. Medi-centre. That's the fancy name. You know what I mean. A raisin farm. A geriatric frat house. Death's own cul-de-sac.

We do a lot of these. Someone finds their house is too much for them. "It's time to simplify," their kids tell them. Time to downsize. Declutter.

It's actually easier for us than a regular move. With a regular move, everything has to go. With downsizing, usually a lot of the big stuff stays behind to be claimed by the relatives. Or they've already swept through to claim some things, or mark others for the donation bins. Especially the books. God, I hate the books. You don't think how quickly they add up in weight, but a small box full of books — one of those banker's boxes (as if a banker would trust any of his valuables to cardboard or give a shit about books) — it weighs a ton. And then if you have a thousand of them — which is what the typical house contains — that's how many trips back and forth? Luckily, it's the first thing that people let go of when they simplify: the library. All those shelves of books they've already read. All that expensive literary wallpaper.

But this move looked easy. I had to reconnoitre the place, put together the estimate, then Kyle and me would come back to do the move itself later in the week.

As we waited for the water to boil, she led me around a bit so she could show me what had to go. A double bed. Simple. Old people usually bought their beds long before the queen and king sizes took over the market — and if they'd lived through the depression, they weren't likely to trade up and throw away a perfectly good headboard and frame. A dining room table. Just four of the eight chairs. Practical.

"I don't even think eight people could fit into my new place," she observed in a kind of jokey way, but I don't think she found it all that funny.

Add two chairs from the living room — not the TV — the son was taking the TV. "I don't watch it much anymore," she said. After that it was just some smaller items. I figured it'd take me and Kyle less than two hours to get everything bundled up and in the truck. The whole move would take less than a half day, even with travel and set-up on the other end. We'd charge her for the full day, finish early, and me and Kyle would have time for beer or two after.

When the kettle called her back to the kitchen, I made my way to the dining room through the living room.

"What about the pictures on the wall?" I called. "How many of these are going?" Pictures can be a pain. They're not heavy, but they need to be wrapped carefully and you have to put them in the truck just right so nothing rests against them.

"I've already boxed up the smaller ones — photographs and the like," she replied, coming in from the kitchen, placing down on the dining room table a plate of shortbread cookies and some sort of loaf. "Of the paintings, there are six on the wall opposite the fireplace that I want to take with me."

"These?" I'd moved to a wall just outside the dining room that contained a number of oil paintings, each around the size of a tabloid newspaper. "Are they real?"

"Yes, those are the ones," she said as she joined me. "My husband painted them. Tea's just steeping. It'll just be a moment."

Typical landscapes, all of them, in rough wooden frames. Good, but clearly amateur. Not that I know much about oil painting, but I could tell by looking at these. The straight edges, the angle of the shadows, they were off just enough to show that the eye was unsure or the hand unsteady, but not enough to be a conscious choice of style.

"Your husband painted these?"

"My late husband, yes. Just."

"Oh. I'm sorry." My apology was spontaneous, although the situation was far from uncommon. She gave me a small smile through compressed lips.

I took a closer look at the pictures, out of respect. Prairie scenes, mostly: wheat fields and weathered barns. But one was of a church, the grounds a little overgrown, the wood of the building largely grey but with the ghost of the original white paint. A graveyard of tilting stones grinning out to a field of grain.

"I know this one. I know this place," I found myself saying.

"St. Andrews. Out by Selkirk."

"I used to work there during the summers — when I was a teenager — cutting the grass and pulling weeds."

"They could use you back there. They've let the weeds get out of control." She looked at me with a sudden intensity I found unnerving, as if looking through murky water to find pebbles below.

"Are you a Ross?" She retrieved the business card I'd given her on my arrival and stared at it.

"Yes."

"Malcolm Ross's boy?"

"No. Malcolm Ross's boy is my dad. Alister."

"Of course. You're much too young. How silly of me." She put the card down on the table next to her cup and saucer.

"William. Bill." I offered my hand, but she had returned to the picture.

"This is from the back of the church looking toward the road. Those stones here —" she offered a bony finger to the picture "— this is where my family is — the Frasers. And my husband — and my youngest boy. Griffins. My great-grandfather Angus Fraser, he built the church — he was a carpenter. Mother and Father farmed six miles over. The Kirks." She pointed to a painting above it — of a farm house in an untended yard. "That's the farmhouse where I grew up. How it looks today, that is. Father would never have allowed it to get run down like that. He liked everything neat. He planted flowers all around the house, and an arbour leading down to the river. The house was white then. Trim. Neat. But now it's empty. Has been for years. And the arbour, well . . ." She turned suddenly from the picture. "I'm Sarah. Sarah Griffin."

I knew this from the work order, from our introduction at the door, but now she offered her hand. I took it in a light grip.

154

Her fingers were thin; the knuckles looked large and angry with arthritis; her bones felt light, like a bird's.

"Bill Ross."

"I shall call you William. Come," she said. "The tea will be ready. I'm sorry it's not my usual. I like a loose leaf — an Oolong. But everything seems to have disappeared. Just the bagged tea for us."

"This is just fine. Thank you."

It was orange pekoe, an inexpensive blend, steeped to a deep brown and the edge of a savage bitterness, re-tamed with milk and two sugars. A bite of buttery shortbread completed the time travel to my mam's kitchen.

"Your husband was a good painter."

"He had some talent. It was his engineering work that paid the mortgage. Forty years with the government before he retired. Of course, I'm glad he painted the church and the homestead. They're special. The others . . . well, he was prolific —" here she leaned in and dropped her voice — the practised motions of gossip, even though the house was empty. "The basement is full of them. Forty years with the government then twenty years as a hobbyist painter. The kids are running out of wall space and won't take any more. But I can't toss them out —" she gave me a knowing look, then resumed her proper posture.

"Still —" I said, but I had nothing more to offer. She filled the silence by laying a slab of butter on a slice of loaf and passing the plate to me.

"Family recipe. Oat and bran. Good for you. I added chocolate, though. And brown sugar. Just because it's good for you doesn't mean you have to suffer."

It was good — very good — but, then, a quarter inch thick slab of butter can't help but elevate anything to perfection.

"You'll meet my son — my youngest, my Gordon — when you come to do the move. He wanted to —" she searches in her bag of diplomacy and finds it somewhat wanting "— supervise."

"An engineer as well?"

"No. A writer. Of sorts. One book."

"Oh. You must be very proud."

"I must admit that I never really understood what he was writing about. My Robert, he was always the reader. He lives two provinces over, my son. Teaches. Used to. It was my son's idea that

I move into something smaller. He wanted me to go into one of those 'complexes,'" she continued, the quotation marks verbal. "But I insisted on my own place, my own apartment. Something older. Something familiar. Five years my Robert has been gone and Gordon feels this place is too big for me."

"Is it?"

"I've lived in this house for forty years. Raised three children here. It's my home." She took a sip of tea. "The stairs are a bother. It takes forever to vacuum. But what else am I going to do to fill my day?"

"You have three children?"

"My daughter is in the arts — theatre, mainly. Sets. Posters. Graphic design." There is a sense of pride in her voice, but also a touch of wariness, as if she was not entirely sure of the safety in offering me this information.

"Another artist? I go to shows now and then. I've probably seen her work."

"I'm sure you have. Sometimes her work is all over town," she says with the briefest wave of her hand. "It's not making her any money, but she's happy. No husband yet. I'd show you the posters, but my son has already packed them all away. I wouldn't know which box to look in. He's taking them all back with him," she says, with an edge of finality.

"Oh, that's all right. Perhaps I'll meet her, too — when I'm back on Thursday to move the furniture."

"No. That's not likely."

"And you have another son?"

"Brendan. He was the youngest. He's not with us anymore."

"Oh. I'm sorry."

"Thank you. It's been some time, but thank you."

Our tea is now finished — mine, at least. Hers sits untouched in her bone china cup.

"Maybe I can take another look through the rooms? You can show me what else I'll be moving on Thursday."

"Of course. Yes. Silly of me. Here I am babbling away, and you have work to do."

We go from room to room — upstairs and down — and she shows me the items I'll need to load up. Each room is ready. Each room has had the small items boxed: the ornaments and trinkets. I only have to worry about the furniture — the big stuff — dressers and the like. Some drawers are partially open, others I check myself. All are empty. Each piece, each box and table, are labelled with tape as to their final destination — the room they'll go to in the new place. These are on green tape. Some have red tape, others blue. These are other drop-off points — other addresses — and I remember that my work order has three locations.

"Shit," I think to myself. My half day is now a full day with the extra travel and bullshit. No beer stop for me and Kyle. At least not on the company's time.

We finish in the master bedroom — her room. Here, as well, everything is boxed and organized. The only evidence that it's occupied still are some clothes in the closet, the carefully made bed, and pictures on the dresser. In silver frames are a line of pictures: a middle-aged man in a suit —the kind of picture you see in the paper to announce an executive promotion — next to that is a younger man in a golf shirt, a holiday shot; then a sort of black-and-white art photo of a dark-haired woman looking off into the distance. Nearby, but separate, in a polished wooden frame, is a boy, perhaps just shy of ten — a school picture: longish hair, a bright rugby shirt, a compressed smile of amusement I remembered from her face.

"It looks like everything is ready."

"Yes. My son and daughter flew in and packed up everything this weekend. Organized everything. Packed up everything I'll need, everything they want. I had them leave a few things out — for my comfort."

Each of the rooms has been surprisingly uncluttered. The number of boxes stacked orderly in each room could not possibly contain everything, the detritus of living — the thousands of mementos and trinkets and just plain junk that accumulate over the years.

"How long did you say you lived here?"

"Forty years. We built this house. We wanted room for the children. Maggie is the oldest. She was three when the house was finished and we moved in. I was expecting Gordon then. We wanted them to have their own rooms. More than we had, growing up."

"Of course."

"We were in a small apartment when we were first married. Robert was just finishing university." Here she touched lightly the frame of the man in the suit. "We had hardly any furniture — barely a dollar left at the end of the month. I remember Robert spreading his assignments on the hardwood floor as he organized them, stretched out, his coffee cup keeping sheets from flying away. Then Maggie was born. Robert got a job. We should have stayed put for a while, I suppose. Taken the safe route. Put a little money aside. But it was such an old building. So dirty. Three flights of stairs. One morning I got up to feed the baby, turned on the kitchen light, and several cockroaches scurried for cover. That's when I said to Robert that we had to move; that I wouldn't raise my children like that. Kids need room. I grew up on a farm — the farm in the picture. We always had room."

"Do you want the boxes moved?"

"Oh, no. Thank you. My son and daughter will take care of those."

"You sure? There aren't many."

She paused for a moment. Looked at me hard, her head tilted toward one shoulder, then looked away slightly, just to the side.

"Have you moved often?" she asked.

"Me? No. Well — when I left home and came to the city. And from my first apartment to where I am now — a few years ago."

"So you didn't really have much."

"Not really. Most of it fit in the back of a friend's pick-up."

She picked up a photograph, the one in the wooden frame — looked at it as she spoke.

"So much we collect. It's like the wind just blows it in, to settle in every crack — to drift into corners. You don't even notice. Old clothes. Vacation souvenirs. Children's toys. Photographs. So many things. No value, really. Except someone touched them once. Someone you knew. Someone you loved. Maybe a long time ago."

She put the photograph back down so gently there was no sound, then turned again to me.

"What is your rule — when you're hired to pack up someone's house — someone's home? What is your rule about what goes in a box and what doesn't? What gets sealed up and what gets discarded?"

"I have no say."

"You don't judge."

"No. It's not my job."

"What would you think if an old woman wanted to keep things — wanted them kept — somewhere. A handful of ties that a man used every working day of his life — every day of his retired life, too, because it was his ritual — whistling a tune as he looked in the mirror — tying a Windsor knot — his annoying tuneless whistling. Or a pipe. No one smokes a pipe anymore. It's of no use to anyone. But its scent is unmistakable. Or a box of toy cars — the miniature kind — metal — chipped from the constant play of a child — before that child grew up to pursue other games. Other childish, hurtful games."

"We'd treat them with as much respect and care as a crystal heirloom."

She laughed a sudden, loud laugh that startled me.

"You sound like your company brochure. *Cherished heirlooms. As if our own.* It's sad to see your life labelled and packed, but it's sadder to see rows of garbage bags ready for pickup. Lying awake in the morning, hearing the screeching caw of brakes as the truck comes to a halt in your back alley — hearing the crushing clatter as it's all tossed into the truck. Imagining them broken into the landfill under the wheels of the equipment."

"They're just things," I offer.

"Yes. That's what I was told. Things. A handful of coins at a yard sale. Not worth the trouble. No room. And I'm a foolish old woman. And it's time for me to go — to downsize."

She seemed to shrink during this. This small woman, barely five-foot at best, had seemed to diminish like a broken doll. Then she drew strength from somewhere. She squared her shoulders, breathed deeply in a ritual I knew she'd practised a thousand times through the years — that I'd seen my own mam use a thousand times. I was reminded of that little church in the painting — so many years in the prairie — the winters — the rough-hewn beams firm against the winds that cut across the fields — once a focus of gathering, of faith, now abandoned — no longer respected, no longer needed, supplanted by the more urgent gods of the day.

"Will this cost much?"

"No. A half day at most. An easy job."

We'd moved back downstairs. I marked everything I needed on my clipboard — all the forms were filled in, boxes checked. I needed a signature, of course, but I suspected it would be the son who would do that. It could wait until Thursday. No rush.

"May I trouble you for some fresh tea?"

"Of course, William. No trouble."

"And another slice of that wonderful loaf."

ONE ON ONE

I stood slowly, knees stiff from the cold, brushed the snow from my pant leg where I'd knelt, pulled my black overcoat tight around me. But instead of turning back to the car, I stopped, caught by a sound in the air. I moved forward toward the small grove of spruce trees at the far side of the building. Listened again. Turned into the sound.

Beyond the tree cover, the fields stretched white and rolling to the horizon. The early morning sun was low and bright, the fresh snow reflecting a pale blue. The cold reached up through my leather shoes, the bright light and cutting wind on my face drawing tears. I rubbed at my eyes with a gloved hand. There, to my left, was the noise again — an almost hollow sound — clicks and slashes, that tugged at my sleeve and cut into my thoughts. I raised my hand to shield my eyes and looked again.

The boy was partially hidden from me by a small rise, but I could tell from the sound, from the way he seemed to glide on the horizon, that he was skating.

I moved through the snow, with heavy, plodding steps, until I was close enough to make out the boy's brown leather skates and the plain wooden stick with *Sherwood* in black block letters, the cloth coat and bright wool toque whose long pointed tail bounced off his shoulder as he turned and wheeled, his breath exploding into the cold with each cut and turn. The rink was nothing but a small patch of ice no larger than a city lot, boarded by the mounds of snow cleared from the area, the surface scoured smooth by the wind.

I stopped at the edge, watched the cursive language the skates left on the clear ice. With a quick turn, the boy stopped suddenly, with that short high scrape and veil of snow I remembered from somewhere, felt as a muscle memory. The boy's face was smooth with youth and red from the cold; he motioned with a heavy leather mitt to the far snow bank. There a stick protruded, blade up, and hanging from it was a pair of skates.

The boy returned to his skating, now making ever increasing circles — laps of the small surface, feet crossing over tight in the corners, four thrusting strides through the straight stretch, then a crouch through the next turn. Then backwards, the low centre, the subtle shift of weight, his head high.

I put one shoe out from the deep bank and onto the ice — the black leather shiny and wet — then the other. Shuffle-stepped across the ice toward the waiting stick, arms out to my side at an awkward angle for balance. Although he didn't turn, I could tell by the silence that the boy was watching, anticipating, patient in his waiting.

At the far bank, I pulled off my gloves, threw off my overcoat and sat down on it to lace up the skates, the boy resuming his circuits. The cold touched my face and my uncovered hands and reached through my sweater. I tugged the laces tight, until my fingers hurt, wrapping the long ends once around the ankle guard before tying the loop.

I stood, unsteady at first, then surprised at how quickly it came back to me — the balance, the smooth shift of weight. I put on my gloves, took the wooden stick from the snow, tested its weight and flex, felt a joy at the perfect symmetry of the overlapping edges of black tape. I tapped the blade on the ice. At the sound, the boy stopped, took a puck from his pocket, and skimmed it to me. It hit my left skate blade, and I caught its rebound on my stick with a forgotten reflex. I moved the puck slowly against the blade, the solid tap resonating up into my hands. I moved forward, the seasons of stiffness melting away, the growing freedom of each glide, as if I had shed the years with my coat.

We set up goals, blocks of snow a stick length apart. Face-off: two taps on the ice, sticks coming together above the puck; third time go — a Morse code instinctive to us. One-on-one. Offer the puck, make 'em commit, snatch it back. Go outside, lean low, forward hand brushing the ice as it sweeps the stick-check aside. Shoulder drop to the outside, cut inside, puck between the legs. Fake the shot. Spin on your backhand. Drive to the net. Drive.

Then teammates. Headman pass. Winger catches up. Give-and-go. Drop pass. Tap-in at the crease. Stick high. The universal sign. Acknowledge the crowd.

"Open, open!" I yelled. "Hum it! Heads up! Stick save! Beats him — like a broken drum — like Mama's old carpet — like a rented mule!" Joyous bravado. Rediscovered laughter. My voice rang out. But something was unsaid. What? I strained to think — to catch the boy's eye — the face, familiar — so like my own, but

162

— what? — but then the puck was mine. No time. The game is all. Later. There'll be time. Later.

And we were Lafleur, Lemaire, Shutt. Savard. Cournoyer. Beliveau. The Forum. Saturday night full. On its feet, the crowd roar like a tide that carries the play. The happiness. We steamed in the sweat of our damp sweaters in defiance of the cold.

I was there again. The world black and white, good versus bad. A religion, a child's grasping at something to give order and meaning. If we win this game, the world will somehow be right. A hat trick means I'll pass the math test. If I can score this goal, this one goal, maybe he'll have a good day. If I can turn this lead pass into a breakaway, maybe he'll be able to come out one more time, to share the frozen Saturday mornings that seemed to stretch out so far — white and rolling to the horizon. Maybe we'll sit together on the couch in the rec room — chips and soft drinks — watch one more game. See the villains of our youth vanquished — with a late goal. A shut-out. But the adult lesson is wishes unanswered. Childish games put aside. Belief lost by pieces, discarded, forgotten on the top shelf of the garage.

I bring my gloved hand back down and I am back in my dark coat, standing again in the snow. I see the boy, from a distance, making those lazy circles, puck tucked between his feet then out again. Spinerama. The Bronx deke.

But now there is no sound. Time is still and hard, the wind like a hand pushing my face away. And when the pain of the cold is too much, I turn back toward the building.

I move stiffly through the trees, snow from the branches slapping at the sleeve of my overcoat, my leather shoes wet. I hunch my shoulders — shiver — then continue through the rows of markers, past the church, to where the car is parked on the gravel road.

A Fall's Reflection

By my count, the man on the lower steps of the art gallery — the man with the shaved head and the long overcoat — had made ten spoon rings in the space of an hour. His overcoat appears to be a dark olive, military issue. One of the epaulets is buttoned securely, but the other is loose and flops in time with his movements — sudden shrugs and flourishes as he bends the metal, as if he's endowing his rings with magic. His sideburns, dyed an intense black, rise from his jaw to an abrupt line at the midpoint of his ears, each of which is pierced with lug bolts through the thin cartilage.

The sun is out, and the late morning has moved to a warm afternoon, but he remains in his long overcoat, regularly lifting his sleeves to wipe his smooth head, which flips his coat open like wings, revealing he is shirtless and muscular, his suspenders made of heavy link chain, rivets securing them to his black canvas pants. His pale skin, almost blue, seems unmarked, oddly smooth and pure.

Many watch; few approach. A man, a security guard from the art gallery I guess by his blue and creased uniform, watches from behind the glass doors above, his arms crossed. His expression is impassive, his posture noncommittal. He could be assessing the risk the spoon man represents; he could be assessing his lunch options.

I know all this because I have been watching spoon man for hours, from not so far away, just across the cobblestone courtyard at an outdoor table of an overpriced café.

I am here watching him because my family has left me. No. That's not true. I have left them. I am supposed to be running errands. I left the hotel to pick things up. I've forgotten now what they were. Razors, maybe. Or exchanging local currency. It doesn't matter. It was a made-up excuse anyway, simple things conflated to seem like they would fill a morning. In fact, if they needed to be done they were resolved in just a few minutes, hours ago, before I found this spot, before I sat down to consider this foreign scene. If they didn't need to be done, then my not doing them will impact no one.

Even with this shallow subterfuge, I am already late. My wife. My daughter. Their expectations. Their demands. So many demands. So many problems — small problems inflated to fill the space — just to get this far, to where we are today. I can't even remember which country this is. I've tried to deduce this by listening to the voices of people passing — to families squabbling in snippets from the distance; or the teasing, laughing, swooping murmurations of teens; or conspiring lovers; or older couples, holding hands, their free hands painting observations as if the sky were a touch screen. I have even watched a dog sit, roll over, bark on command, in this foreign country, in this foreign language. But I am no further ahead.

Italy, I think. Yes. "If this is Tuesday, we must be in Italy," as the old tourist joke goes, and I am left with the realization that the dog understood more Italian than I do.

But I sit. And observe. And the weather warms, the girls wearing less and less, like a falling of leaves in reverse to the cues of the environment.

At some point they will miss me, my wife and my daughter. Perhaps because they will need something. My daughter, to find the shops. My wife, the museums. Or perhaps just because I said I would be back. Together, alone together, they will focus their energies on their differences, only coming to common ground should I reappear. I suppose I am the glue whose absence allows the cracks between them to reopen.

No. Perhaps that's unfair. But the sun is so warm on my face. The distant girls at the fountain so pretty. Bobbing their heads together like pigeons, in whispered conversations with their BFFs — the whispers for effect only, as the risk of common language for any eavesdropping tourists is not within the balance of probability. There I go, thinking like an analyst again.

The weight, the stability of the stone buildings that fortress the circumference of this space, the steps rising up from the plaza, represent antiquities that have survived the erosion of the years far better than I. No building today, no rising monument of steel and glass, could compete, their height greater but cheap compensation for the intensity that encircles me.

And oh, the warm sun on my face. I have spent the hours precisely shifting my chair, my position, to maintain the angle, finally seeing the inevitable: that the sun's shadow — the shadow of the adjacent building — will soon cut its razor edge across the café. And in the shadows, the sun will become something only for observation. The perspective will be exaggerated, elongated, until a choice must be made: to move to another perspective or to move on. To return.

The origin of my ennui, my malaise, was so casual. I think that makes it worse, but I guess it's so often that way. At supper last night — our first night here — Zöe said it. As we passed down the grand stairs of our hotel to meet her mother in the dining room, I had commented that it felt as if we were walking into history. She replied that finally she would have something to counter her English teacher, who had spent all last term bragging about his trip to New York in April.

Why should I care? Teachers go to New York. Male teachers go to New York. Even male teachers who had once had an affair with my wife may go to New York. Perhaps even in the same April as my wife is there on business. Life is full of just such coincidences, and Zöe — Zee, as she now insists upon being called — would have seen no resultant hesitation in my step, only how my hand trailed easily along the smooth, marble balustrade. But my mind had turned to other histories, other pasts.

Do I love my wife? Am I merely comfortable with her? These are the questions for a sunny fall day in a European plaza. Because I haven't got the energy to confront her. Not again. To do so — to hear again the excuses, the mea culpas that had sounded then like accusations. She felt lost, she'd said, sought something I wasn't providing, a need I wasn't fulfilling. "I did this because you made me feel . . ." picking a word from her thesaurus of blame. To confront her now would mean that we're over. It would end the trip. Would ruin dinner. Spoil everything. And I would be blamed for my poor timing. So I was prepared to continue playing the secret fool — to not have my foolishness made known, made public. Zöe. Zee.

Does she know? Does she suspect? Did she say this to bait me? She has grown more aloof recently, and, if so, is it due to her contempt for me, for my weakness? Or is she just a teenager? Is she a believer in the purity of love, as the young so often start out to be, and does she hate me for my inability to fight? She made no further reference. At dinner she merely begged for free time to visit the shops, more spending money, a chance to have some wine with dinner — a sip of the more liberal drinking laws. And we had calmly acquiesced — shared a moment of lax parenting. We. Katherine and me.

Katherine. I remember when I first met her — my awkwardness, my earnestness. Laughter as a form of intimacy. My desire, at the time, my taste for dark bags beneath the eyes of pale and slender women. Where had I read that? From my studies at the time, perhaps. Part of the assigned reading — the literature that did not prepare me for life the way I had been promised. Yes, I had loved her. But then we all carry around a memory that isn't true.

But that was so long ago. I thought I'd settled into my age — that time had smoothed the sharp edges. Until this, I was so much more comfortable, more confident and contented with myself — the stable inertia of my career, unlike Katherine's fast-rising ambition.

Money sits in the small saucer on the table. Change. Oddly sized, bright bills and small, heavy coins. I have been holding a coin in my hand for how long I don't know. Rolling it. Enjoying its weight, its substance. Soothed by the predictable geometric angles of its edge.

What had she said that handful of months ago? After the first wave had passed from her earlier indiscretion. "We need to get away." I remember as she stood by the window on that rainy night — the reflection on her face of the drops running down the panes, looking like the tears she should have been shedding, the impatient tapping of the rain on the glass.

But we are civilized. We do not shout. We are educated, logical. Detached. We argue with our inside voices. When you need to distance yourself from a problem, from a choice, you travel.

The waiter returns again, hovers for a moment. He is dressed in black: black vest, black pants, black tie. His white apron extends from his waist to the top of his black shoes. It must be restrictive, this impractical costume of his profession, but the tourists expect it — how it speaks of history, a past that no longer exists, if it ever did. I nod my head, and he reaches for the saucer of change. That is the extent of our communication. But he hesitates in his motion — his attention pulled momentarily to the spoon man, or maybe to the young girls at the fountain as they raise a coin to their lips before tossing it into the water with their wish — and I see a tattoo on his arm, exposed by his reach for the saucer — a sleeve of colour and statement hidden beneath the clean white shirt. I look away — at the coin I've kept, the simple number on the front, the obverse crowded with letters and a date, and the profile of someone long dead. Then the waiter is gone.

"Are we okay?" was my reply to her.

"I feel that you're no longer on my side," she'd said. How typical of her to make it about sides. How typical of me to focus on this.

Where to go, then. Europe, she'd suggested. The grand tour. Distance the solution. And she made the plans, the arrangements, the reservations — offered it up to Zee as a gift. Four weeks.

Zee had sat between us on the flight, plugged into her headphones most of the time, flipping through fashion magazines until finally she slept. Katherine, too, finally nodded off, an open book limp in her lap, the pages drifting with her shallow breathing. I ordered another scotch from the steward and watched the movie on the TV screen, the earphones dangling on my armrest, images flickering unfocused.

Now my phone sits on the table, upside-down, off. Impotent. It's a device, meant to increase the connection between people — call, text, social media — but, really, it has sliced human interaction so thinly as to be translucent and unrecognizable. It has merely removed our responsibility for clarity. Increased the number of ways we can be misunderstood.

Just as I'm considering confronting him — my ring maker — consider the option of replacing my simple gold band with a twist of his recycled silver — a game to see how long before the substitution is noticed — the spoon man kneels to pack up his tools and materials in a canvas bag. It takes but a moment, and he is striding away, purposefully. And I realize that I don't want him to go. That I need him to remain at his station, tall and oblivious to the heat of the day. For with him gone, I must make my own decision to stay or to go.

I rise, push my dead phone into my pocket, and move to the fountain. The central bronze sculpture is of a powerful antique god, with flowing beard and trident. Beneath are gargoyles at regular intervals spitting out water from their mocking mouths. I want to reach into one, into the void, like Gregory Peck in Roman Holiday, the water washing over my hand and forearm as I jump back with childlike glee. But instead I simply toss my phone into the fountain, without a wish. It settles quickly among the coins, its ripple soon lost in the surface noise of the water.

When I turn to go, I see that someone has taken the place of the ring maker, and the randomness of his location is shattered. It is a busker stand, regulated by a distant bureaucrat, relinquished on schedule, the rebellious look of the spoon man likely no more than a costume, an affectation, the entire effect curated by the adjacent gallery.

It is a woman this time, dressed in flowing fabrics and soft colours of mustard and field flowers. She carries nothing but a bright handkerchief, which she places on the cobblestones in front of her and weighs down with a coin at each corner.

She steps back, clasps her hands together, and begins to sing.

The song is in Italian, I think, something operatic or perhaps antique and traditional. She's a soprano, her unaccompanied voice touches the high notes so lightly — soft, lingering, loving, warming, tender. The song has a necessity, each note leading to the next as if no note could be otherwise. And I feel pulled into this song I do not understand — travelling along the melody until the peripheral of my vision collapses inward, until my wife and my daughter — until Katherine and Zöe — are gone. I am drawn into this song by its beauty, by its simplicity, until the years are falling to dust and nothing else in the world matters. The buildings rise and curve, joining in the sky above me to dome the square, and I disappear, the coin dropping to the stones where I'd stood.

My last glimpse, far below, in a single bright flash of the low reflected sun, is of myself, standing in a cobblestone square, sobbing as the tourists move away in ripples and the afternoon shadows sweep over me.

A Limited Run

Auguste was of the opinion that the fringe festival had devolved to contain far too many 'one-man shows,' and that this distracted audiences from how good his own one-man show was.

After all, Auguste (his real name) had been doing his show almost since day one — when the festival began over thirty years ago. And, no, it was not static, his show. He was proud that he had changed it over the years — albeit somewhat grudgingly — polishing it, refining it, slipping in new jokes with current references: the correct prime minister, for example, the right war, that crazy pop singer — the woman — you know, the one who substitutes vocal gymnastics for lyrical quality. And the popular athletes — all millionaires — remembering to link the right team with the correct sport. So many bizarre names to mispronounce.

But these were the sorts of changes that sophisticated audiences liked — that kept the show fresh and edgy — even though he was not fond of edgy himself, and freshness was so much work. And people were so quick to be offended these days. No more wife jokes, or foreign accent jokes. No more lispy innuendoes.

But people came to see *him*, after all. He had his regulars. He had his increasingly monochromatic groupies.

True, he was almost sixty now, and the happy, roly-polyness that had charmed and captivated his earlier audiences had progressed to something nearer obesity, a drooping looseness that necessitated him cutting much of the physical comedy that tended to just leave him sweaty and wheezing — that caused some in the front few rows to flinch from the fine mist that enveloped them, its imminent arrival foretold through the pearl-like dance of droplets in the reflection of the footlights.

More polishing, that's all that was needed. Build on the core strength of classic comedy with a polished veneer of the contemporary — that was what the audiences wanted nowadays — expected — as they matured with him. A heavy dose of the classics. That was his formula. And that would bring them back, though what had driven them away in the first place was a mystery.

The economy. That handful of misinformed reviews. The growing vulgarity of the festival performers as a whole.

And the heat.

Was it getting hotter each summer? Perhaps a global warming joke would add some edginess, although he knew little of the politics and even less of the science.

He pulled a handkerchief from his pocket. "Am I the last one to use a handkerchief," he wondered, as he blotted at his forehead which had grown over the years, much like the empty seats pushing back his receding audience.

But the handkerchief was part of his costume. Like his pants, black; his frilled tuxedo shirt, white (or white-ish), open at the collar; his red suspenders, the strained clips clinging to his pants like fingernails on a cliff edge, brimming with the potential energy of a deadly projectile should they surrender to the inevitability of physics; his black jacket, with shining patches and greying lines at the cuffs; and on his head a hat — 'porkpie' they called it once — black, with a bright yellow band and a long red ostrich feather (or the polyester equivalent). If you had not seen the outfit when crisp and new with his act, you would have assumed he possessed an ironic self-awareness on the cutting edge of humour. And if you had seen his act — just the first moments would suffice — you would know that irony and self-awareness were strangers to him.

At the start of it all, when main venues were easily obtained, and audiences were young in their expectations, he had done well. Well enough to leave behind his sales job at the dealership for two weeks in the summer. Well enough to return the next year and the next. Soon the sales job was gone — his aggressive chumminess no longer in vogue — but his show remained. He had his following. Local notoriety had been enough to parlay into occasional office parties or Christmas reviews, or Rotary fundraisers — what passed as suburban stardom in a small-to-medium-sized city.

Then came the indignity of the waiting list in year nine of the festival. The scramble to find his own venue since — a variety of the dark and pre-condemned — finally settling, in the last several years, as a regular upstairs in a pre-Great War block — the small brick space above the cheese shop, where the heat and the humidity that served so well to ripen the downstairs product melted his audience. The space that fit exactly forty-one seats for anyone keen on challenging geometry or the limits of personal space. It was only two blocks off the main festival site, but that had to be a factor, he was sure. No one liked to stray too far from the site for the late nighttime slots foisted on him after the other acts — the acts who seemed so much better connected to the owner, to the festival organizers — only after they had cherrypicked the best times.

At present, Auguste is staring at a telephone pole — a strategic pole at the centre of the site. He has a poster in his hand, a staplegun in his side jacket pocket. He had been deciding the optimum position for his poster. There is no space left — there is never any space left, such is the optimum position of this pole. The vaguely moral dilemma is whose poster to cover over. The local high school production of *Godspell*? The Gynecology Professional's Association production of *The Vagina Monologues* (done with half the cast in masks, the other half in stirrups)? Another Brechtian cabaret? The revival tribute of the 80s punk rock band Arsenic Machine, starring the one original member not dead or still serving the full term of their sentence? He finally decides upon an improv show. But which? They had all become indistinguishable to him — cute, pun-ish names, overtly pornographic.

But as he holds his poster up to check the position in the advantageous mid-afternoon sun, he flicks a corner of torn poster off, revealing the anthropological layers of posters from previous years, exposing splashes of colour he finds unsettlingly familiar.

His poster is a closeup of his face in full smile, the title, the location and the times in large, italicized Comic Sans font. He places his stack of posters down on the grey asphalt and reaches forward with a tentative hand. With a dirty fingernail, he picks away at a rusted staple to free a triangle of weathered paper. He holds it up to his face. His slightly rheumy eyes are far from as keen as they had been but, still, the image is familiar.

The poster is from his show. He can see that now. A show ten years ago. He can tell by the colour and the small portion of bowtie. His posters changed little over the years — usually just the border colour, rotated through the wheel of primary options. But when he started, he wore a bowtie, large and flowered. He'd only dropped it a few years ago — because of the heat; because it required that he button his collar.

He looks again at the pole, at the spot where the remnant had been unearthed. He reaches out again and presses his forefinger against the spot where the remnant had been unearthed, feels the soft give of the posters that tells him that the wood itself is an inch or more beneath — that in placing his poster up he will be driving the staple through years of posters, back through time.

He peels away the Brecht poster, then last year's *Improvapalooza* beneath it, finding his own layered history: weathered displays of his own face, or remnants of it, getting younger even as the paper yellows. The bottom piece is little more than a ghost, barely recognizable as a face — as his face — the paper rotten and crumbling to his touch.

He stands for a moment in his disquiet. His thought drifts to his performance space — of his tech rehearsal the day before. There are four shows sharing both the space and the technician. He remembers the narrow stairs, looking up to the walls closing in in the darkening perspective, feeling the air temperature and humidity increase with each upward step, the assault of decay and fermentation.

His show is mostly lights-up/lights-down, but he likes to meet the tech. He's always felt that he had a special bond with the technical people, that he showed them respect and they, in turn, knew him for the professional he is. But this year it's a young guy — can't be more than eighteen or nineteen. Spiked hair. His earlobes stretched so open by black, plastic rings that Auguste felt he could put his thumb through — could use it to open coke bottles. Ha! He could use that in his act, maybe. The kid doesn't get the humour of Auguste's act. Doesn't smile. Doesn't laugh. Doesn't even try. Spends the time texting. By the end Auguste had simply mumbled his way through the last fifteen — finally standing in the glare until the kid noticed and gave the lights down.

He'd left the theatre feeling uneasy, and decided to stop at a local coffee shop to treat himself to one of those foreign sounding drinks — more milk and syrup than coffee, but comforting just the same. The place was all wooden tables and mismatched cast-off chairs, and crowded — but he found a spot near the window. The table was wobbly, which had annoyed him. He'd looked down and found that he'd dislodged a folded paper someone had wedged under a leg. And as he bent over to put the paper back in place, he'd recognized it as one of his show handbills that he'd been distributing all day.

He was still holding it when the child in the satanic T-shirt arrived to take his order. But misunderstanding, she'd taken the paper from his hand and wedged it back beneath the table leg, flashing him a triumphant 'that'll fix it' smile through her piercings.

He stands for several more seconds at the pole, feeling the hot August sun raise sweat on the back of his neck, dampening his jacket.

"You done, old timer?"

He looks up blankly from the rusted staple and stab of coloured paper in his open palm.

"Wakey, wakey. This is your cue to exit, stage right."

There are three of them. Young. Hair of varying lengths and colours. The girl wears makeup based upon sharp contrasts of black and white, her eyes blinks of charcoal. The two men — boys, really — are in baggy shorts and T-shirts, the words and symbols on them a whirl of the indecipherable. One has a red beard. He is the one talking, a smile in his tone, a grin on his face, pointing to the feather in Auguste's hat.

"Come on, Robin Hood. It's not your pole. Sharing, okay. Some of us get to have our square foot, too."

He swings a blue backpack off his shoulder and takes a poster from it. He holds it up for Auguste to see. Red Beard's tone is a comic Tarzan now.

"Poster. We put up poster now."

The girl laughs. Jane laughs. The other man grunts like an ape, his stance crouched, his arms swinging.

Auguste says nothing, but looks at their poster. The group is called 'Post No Bills,' obviously a joke so they can put their posters up on the decorative lamp posts that now line the gentrified streets, believing that they are pushing back against 'the man.' The block letters shout about an improv musical, the picture of the three of them in poses, caught in mid-song. All youth. All energy. A main stage. They'll sell out, he's sure. No question. They couldn't help but sell out.

"I can tell from your quick repartee that improv is your game as well. Eventually."

He hears a dog bark somewhere. He thinks about storytelling — how stories evolve — how with each telling, things became more intense. A dog becomes bigger or growls more menacingly. A woman becomes more beautiful. A situation more fraught. And he wonders if his memory is doing that to him. If his past crowds were never that big; if they didn't laugh as hard; if he was not actually —

Red Beard moves past Auguste, nudges him so he stumbles back two or three steps. Jane catches him by the shoulder and twirls him in a brief dance, then steps back with Auguste's hat in her hand, sweeping it in a low, Shakespearean bow. She holds it out, as if to play a game of keep-away, but he turns from her and watches Red Beard place their poster on top of Auguste's past, driving a staple through the corner of their poster, into what would have been Auguste's eye beneath.

Auguste feels a sudden stab of pain and a sickness, in his chest and his stomach.

Now it's Red Beard's turn to stare. Auguste shivers for a dozen seconds, suddenly cold and sweating, causing the others to exchange looks — looks but no movement, until Jane steps forward and places the feathered hat back on his head, reaches out as if to touch his arm, then pulls back and steps close to the other two.

Auguste is seized with a sudden urge to move, a frantic need to act. His show. Of course. He has to get to his show.

He pushes past the group, past the pole, the staple and remnant of paper falling from his limp left hand. He moves quickly up the sidewalk toward the centre of the festival, toward the noise of the midway.

"Hey! You forgot your posters, old man!"

Red Beard picks up the stack of posters from where Auguste had left them on the ground, but Auguste doesn't look back, doesn't hear their laughter, doesn't see Red Beard drop the stack in the nearest bin. He has a show to do. He feels suddenly old and ridiculous, but with a rising sense of urgency. He has a show to do.

But now he is at the centre — the streets are already crowded with people — gawkers more interested in cheap beer and greasy food than theatre. The air is thick with the smell of spilt beer, and sugary treats, and meat frying and the sick of someone's child — the coloured balloon in their small hand marking the moment of their sweet, pinkish vomit.

He tries to push on, but crowds block him, lingering in rings around the street performers. Flames leap high, spin, are caught, then tossed upward again. A street magician — sparkling vest, bright suspenders, bright patter — cheats him as objects disappear with a wave of his hand.

The voices are loud. The people oppressive. He stumbles against a woman wearing a bizarre costume of bright bangles, then backward into a stroller, is tangled briefly in a dog leash. He frees himself, turns to run, but the other way is blocked by a crowd watching a girl in a wheelchair playing an accordion, the coins tossed into the open case in front of her sounding a percussion to her sentimental melody.

He ducks down an alleyway, past the stand of bright plastic portable toilets, then down an adjoining alley.

Finally, he's alone.

He stops, searches for his breath, rests the back of his head against the cool brick of a building as he feels the summer heat return. He opens his eyes, and for a moment he thinks it's just the sudden glare of the sun, the way his vision is lost in the intensity, details pixelated, his peripheral sharpened down to a narrow cone. But he is also aware of the pain in his knees as he slides down into the gravel of the alley.

And he is tired. Too tired. The show feels like a burden weighing on his back, pushing on his chest, shrieking through his shoulders into his arms.

If he could just put it down for a moment. Rest. Catch his breath, which is now reduced to shallow gasps between the pain. If he could just lie on his back for a moment. And then he is. And now the sky is so blue high above, a distant banner beckoning past the grey of the buildings. One arm still rests against the brick, the other trails in the damp gravel. His hat has rolled off to one side, the ostrich feather against the damp like a blood trail.

He begins to claw ineffectually at the collar that is already open, to loosen the tie that is not there, when a noise quiets him — so distant but recognizable, like rain on the horizon. It swells, bouncing off the walls of the alley before resting on him, covering him. Comforting him. And he feels a calmness as he melts into the sound, floating for the briefest of moments on the applause and laughter of the far crowd.

He remained there — held over, if you will — for three days. Not waiting to be found, for several people had walked by, clutching their common assumption for the presence of a prone man in the shadows of an alley in this neighbourhood. Not waiting to be found, but to be finally acknowledged.

Acknowledgements

To create something new is not a solitary process. And, thankfully, I was never alone in this journey.

"A Fall's Reflection" won first place in Freefall Magazine's short fiction competition and appeared in the Fall 2024 issue. "Conversations with Cows" began life as a short story and was rewritten as a play for the 2024 Edmonton Fringe Festival. This version represents the transformation of that play back to a short story. "Life in a Bottle" was published as part of the *Bristol Short Story Prize Anthology Volume 14* (2021), after placing in their short fiction competition. An earlier version of "A Life Indivisible" was published in the Spring 2021 edition of *Freefall Magazine*, under the title "By the Numbers," after placing in their short fiction competition. An earlier version of "Coffee Break" was broadcast as part of CBC Radio's Alberta Anthology. Thank you to the judges and the audiences who provided validation for the work.

Thank you to the writers in residence who provided encouragement and feedback on some of the stories: Ian Williams on "Stick People," while the University of Calgary's writer in residence, and Susie Moloney on "A Fall's Reflection," while writer in residence for Edmonton Public Library. Thanks to the team at University of Calgary Press – Aritha van Herk, Brian Scrivener, Helen Hajnoczky, and Alison Cobra – for their trust and guidance, to Melina Cusano for her cover design, and to editor Naomi K. Lewis for her kind comments and tough questions. And to my daughters, Jessica and Emma, for constantly inspiring me with their energy, humour and unique takes on the world.

But my greatest thanks goes to Leslie Greentree. It was she who encouraged me to write (and rewrite) the stories. And it was she who told me I had a manuscript. She is my first and most trusted reader. Without her, this book would not exist (and I would be but a shadow of my current self).

Photo Credit: Leslie Greentree

BLAINE NEWTON is an award-winning playwright, comedy and short fiction writer, actor and sometime engineer. His plays have been produced across western Canada, and his short fiction has been published in magazines and anthologies, and featured on CBC and CKUA radio. He lives in Edmonton with his wife, Leslie Greentree. *Rag Pickers* is his first short story collection.

 **BRAVE & BRILLIANT SERIES**

SERIES EDITOR: Aritha van Herk, Professor, English, University of Calgary
ISSN 2371-7238 (PRINT) ISSN 2371-7246 (ONLINE)

Printed by Imprimerie Gauvin
Gatineau, Québec